HAVE YOU HEARD ABOUT KAREN?

KARIN AHARON

To my friends.
I could never have done this without you.

Have You Heard About Karen?

Karin Aharon

Edited by Sharon Honeycutt

Contact: karinaharon8@gmail.com

❀ Created with Vellum

ONE BRIGHT DAY (OR NOT)

TARA

"So, what's the next step in this battle?" I ask my lawyer, feeling like a boxer before a title match, except that my opponent has been sleeping next to me every night for the past thirteen years.

"First of all, tell no one. Ethan must not hear about it too soon. The element of surprise is important," she answers without a hint of emotion. When I think of it, I realize I've never seen her smile.

"Anything else?"

"I suggest you start organizing every document that might be relevant, such as those regarding shared assets, information about his business – all the things that need to be addressed in the agreement. And try to see if he's hiding any funds or other assets from you."

"Okay, thank you. Is there anything else you need from me now?"

"You need to sign this power of attorney." She places the document with my name typed on it in front of me and lays a blue pen next to it.

I sign and smile at her, but she doesn't smile back at me. Maybe she'll smile when she gets her fee.

"Do you think he'll cooperate with the mediation?" she asks, typing rapidly without looking at me. "It will make it easier for both of you."

I remember my last conversation with Ethan. He looked at me like he didn't understand the words coming out of my mouth, as if we were speaking two different languages. He didn't say much, other than occasionally groaning at me. As usual.

He always thinks he knows everything, but he'll soon find out he doesn't.

Too bad for him.

RYLIE

"We don't need a big event or anything like that, babe. A small wedding in my parents' backyard will be fine with me," I say, resting my head on Noah's chest as we curl up in bed while he reads his emails. He strokes my head gently, and I close my eyes.

"It's not the size of the event that matters, it's the event itself," Noah says. "You know how I feel about remarrying now. It's not the right time."

"When will it be the right time? I'm also a part of it, you know. What about what I want? Why do I have to keep waiting?"

Noah sighs and his gentle caressing stops. "What's wrong with us the way we are now?"

"It's like I'm your lover, not your wife. We have two boys, but we're still considered single."

"I don't understand what you want from me. A fucking piece of paper? Is that what you need? You're acting like a little whining girl who needs a certificate to show her mommy."

"You're so annoying! It's not the paper I need, it's the feeling that we're a family – a real family. It will send Danielle the message that I'm here to stay. Don't you understand?"

Noah props himself up on his elbow and looks at me so that I can see the anger in his eyes. "No, I don't. You're the mother of my children. My partner. We live together and we are a family. That should be enough for now."

"But it's not enough for *me*."

"This isn't the time to talk about it," Noah says. "What the hell do you want from me?"

"I want the truth! I want you to admit it's all because of Danielle. We moved to this boring neighborhood because of her. I changed my whole life because of her. But with all due respect to your daughter, we have two boys and it matters to them that their parents aren't married."

"They don't care at their age about our marital status. What's wrong with me wanting Danielle to grow up a little bit before I change her life again? The divorce was hard on her, and she shouldn't have to handle anything more right now."

"Just so you know, I can't go on like this. I'm not going to put my life on hold just because your top priority is your daughter. I won't allow her to push me aside again and again." I stand up and stomp from our bedroom, imagining Noah remaining in bed with a surprised look on his face.

I will not give up. I will not let his annoying, sassy child ruin my life. I'm fed up with Noah's waiting game.

KAREN

It's getting warmer, so I decide to arrange my clothes for summer. Opening the doors of the wardrobe, I stand in front of it in despair. It's packed with clothes I hardly ever wear anymore because I have nowhere to go.

I pull out a pile of tailored trousers that still smell of dry cleaning. I don't know what to do with them. Maybe it's time to move the whole pile to the top shelves. Instinctively I reach for the chair but then I remember I shouldn't climb anything as I might fall. I return the pile and open the shoe drawer.

When I was still working, I wore high heels every day to compensate for my lack of height. Without them, I felt like a schoolgirl dressing up as a programmer. I take out my worn yet useable black pair of pumps. The last time I wore them, it felt like I was walking on a bed of nails. Sadly, I put them – my favorite pair – in a plastic bag.

In between my dresses, I find too many unworn blouses. Taking out the blue silk, the one with the small purple flowers on it, I gently caress it and remember how it felt on my skin. I was wearing it the day I learned about my promotion to team leader, when Will, the CEO, shook my hand. We were in his

office, and I was trembling with excitement. All the plans I had
...

Only now do I realize how much I enjoyed dressing so
smartly for the office. My outfit helped me get into character.
My team admired me – and not only because of what I wore. I
was sharp and efficient, unlike my status at home.

In front of the mirror, I pull on the blouse, dressing up
again. At first, I don't recognize myself. With every passing year,
more and more grey hairs have joined my loose blond ponytail.
When I was working, I pulled my hair back tightly, like the
super-nanny. If she could see me now as a full-time mother, she
would give *me* a time-out.

My stomach's still flabby and marked from the third pregnancy. I'm still thin, but I look as if I'm four months pregnant,
though the big sweaters I wear usually hide it well. I see the
wondering looks people give me: *Is she pregnant or...* I'm not
blind yet.

Yes. The blouse still fits me. The question is – do *I* still fit
the blouse?

I put it back on the hanger and close the doors of the
wardrobe – and the doors on my previous life.

ALMOST ONE YEAR EARLIER

1

KAREN

"Yesterday was lovely. We went to a great restaurant and everything was delicious. Adam bought me a bracelet with the girls' names engraved on it."

"Sounds fun! I saw your post on Facebook and you looked great – not a day over thirty-nine!" Tara laughs, and in the background, I hear baby Emma crying. "We must celebrate your birthday somewhere fancy, and soon."

"That would be great," I reply, knowing that the chances of us celebrating soon are very slim. We're both so busy, we can barely talk on the phone or meet up, except for when we accidentally bump into each other in the parking lot or at our children's school. If we weren't living on the same street, that wouldn't happen either.

Tara was a bit more available in the evenings before Emma was born a few months ago, on those rare days when she returned from her office early. We loved just sitting on the sidewalk between my house and hers, sipping the occasional glass of red wine. We watched the women who power-walked in the evening, gossiped about our husbands, and rested for a while from the incessant noise at home.

If we escaped too early in the evening, within fifteen minutes someone from either house was shouting, "Mom!" and the retreat was sadly over. We'd part with a quick goodbye and a promise of another meeting, which usually took place, coincidentally, on the same sidewalk, but without the comfort of the red wine.

"Sorry, I have to go," I tell Tara now. "I'm late and a client's already waiting for me." I literally run to my office, put my bag down, and take out my laptop. The silly unicorn sticker Olivia decorated it with is still there. So unprofessional.

"No worries, honey. Talk to me later."

Tara hangs up, and I take a deep breath, put on a big smile, and open the wide door to the conference room. The long black wooden table in the middle of the room is surrounded by grey leather chairs, and as I enter the room, Danny, the new client, rises from one and puts down his phone next to his state-of-the-art laptop. No unicorn. I smile.

"Good morning," he says. "The traffic was crazy today, right?"

I don't want to admit that the real reason I'm late this morning is Amelia, who couldn't decide if she wanted to wear the pink skirt or the red one. This fateful decision delayed me at home exactly the fifteen minutes I needed to avoid the traffic to the city.

I notice that Will, the CEO, tries to hide his eye-rolling while presenting me as the team leader in charge of the new software project. I've been working in the company for ten years as a programmer, and in the last year, I managed to reach the desired title "head of development team." It wasn't a big change, but a few young developers – by "young" I mean full of joy and without any wrinkles or stretch marks – now work under me. On some days they have no motivation to invest beyond the minimum requirements of the job. There is something spoilt in this generation; they seem to have more fun and fewer obligations. *How come we never thought of this?* I've caught myself wondering more than once.

The meeting with Will and Danny ends, and I walk back into my office, which is, in fact, a workspace encased by glass walls containing five desks and a grey round table in the center. Zero privacy. It's like working in a shared aquarium, though I'm not sure whether it's a fish or a shark tank.

Mia calls every day when she returns home from school, often to either whine about her homework or complain about the food I left her. Because everyone in the office can hear her screaming even without the speaker and I don't want my team to be part of the conversation, I usually go out to the smelly smoking balcony as soon as I see Mia's name appear on the screen. If I don't, I can see my team's looks range from sympathetic to contemptuous. And I can't blame them. Their manager can't manage her own home.

These frustrating conversations with Mia make me feel guilty that I'm not there for her as I should be – as I once thought I would want to be. The mom waiting for the girls at home after school with a fresh lunch on the table. The mom who listens to their stories about their annoying teachers and helps them with their homework.

That mom is not me.

It took me a while to admit that being that kind of mother wasn't for me. I really tried, but I wasn't good at it. The house chores are boring; I find little challenge in folding laundry or preparing dinners that require more than one pot. At my age, I can admit that I can't handle the title of "full-time mom." Plus, I love my girls, so why would I give them my own cooking?

Instead, I'm here in this aquarium as much as I can be, more concerned about my clients than about my children. If I wasn't so excited about what I do, I might have chosen to look for a part-time job, but I don't want to give up my status and my salary. I struggled so hard to get where I am today. I feel like I'm in the exact place I'm meant to be.

I usually come home around 4:00 p.m., but twice a week I stay late. On those days I feel much calmer. There's no pressure to arrive on time to daycare, no separating screaming girls in petty quarrels over a pink hairbrush with the unicorn, and I even get to drink hot coffee and visit the bathroom without shouting "wait" or "leave her alone" through the closed bathroom door.

This work-home balance might not suit everyone, but it works great for me. Ilene, my mother-in-law, for example, wasn't happy about it. She is generally dissatisfied with me, though, so her opinion doesn't count. I once believed that as long as Adam's happy, she can't utter a word about it. I was so wrong.

There are days when I play with the thought of opening my own software development company. A small one, from home maybe, eliminating the hour-long drive every morning and cursing the traffic every five minutes. There would be no lazy employees who only want to cut corners whenever possible so they can get home in time to watch some boring games.

But being at home all day doesn't seem so appealing. I love meeting people and spending time outside the house. I like the thrill of a good presentation, the admiration I get from management and clients. All of it.

Somedays, though, I feel like I'm not doing anything right. I never finish all my tasks when I have to leave the company early, and when I get home, it's as if I arrived in the middle of a play and I don't know my lines. I'm just lost.

My cooking is a bug I just can't fix. A few weeks ago, Tara gave me a recipe for spaghetti and meatballs. Sounds easy, right? Wrong! First, I went to our local grocery and asked Sammi which "green stuff" was the basil. He laughed in my face because he thought I was kidding. I wasn't. So embarrassing.

Then I tried cooking according to the recipe, and I have the burn mark to prove it. I really tried, but the meatballs were so hard Olivia almost lost her tooth trying to eat them. It was a total disaster. Adam kissed me on my head as he ordered pizza for dinner.

Sometimes I wonder what I really want to do with my life. Maybe it's part of my midlife crisis. Who knows? I'm thirty-nine and a day, so I'm entitled to a midlife crisis.

Last night we went out for dinner with Adam's parents, Ilene and Jacob, and they invited my younger brother Steven as well. He looks nothing like me, taking after our dad – he's tall, dark, and curly-haired and has dimples. I got Mom's fine, bright blonde hair and her tiny body. Ilene and Jacob (mainly Jacob, if we want to be accurate) tried to make me feel welcome, but all these events remind me of those who aren't here with us – my own parents.

Adam promised me that next year we'll do something special for my fortieth birthday, that it won't be another dinner with his parents. I'm considering a short getaway to the Maldives or Seychelles. Somewhere exotic. Tara and Ethan traveled to the Maldives for her fortieth birthday and had the best time (they continue to share their Facebook posts from that trip), but unlike us, they could afford the best hotel on the best island. We hope our whole trip will cost only as much as they paid for one night. We must find a cheaper option.

Teasing me a while ago, Adam said that we'll find ourselves camping on the beach in the Maldives if it's up to me, but I believe we can find a vacation we won't pay for until I'm forty-one. We have almost a year to plan my birthday, and I have to survive the next year without losing my mind.

Since we're about to release a new version of one of our products, I have to stay late in the office today. There are several bugs we just can't overcome, even though my whole team is working on it around the clock.

"Do you want to contribute to the gift for Dave?" Anna asks as she returns from another smoke break. My best developer, Anna has brown hair down to her shoulders, which reminds me of Dora the Explorer, and thick brown glasses. She works harder than the rest and is eager to prove herself. She has no sense of humor, and she's a bit weird (and not just because she drinks tea with milk, and maybe some vodka). I can definitely see her replacing me when I move on to a more senior position.

"How much this time?" I ask reluctantly. I don't know Dave so well, but that doesn't matter. I'm expected to contribute to the collective gifts.

"A tenner each," Anna replies, and I hand her the money. In a company as big as ours, these gifts add up to a considerable amount every year, but I have no choice.

My phone vibrates on my desk.

"Will you be joining us tonight?" Rylie WhatsApps, and I realize I totally forgot that I signed up for her evening group workout. I consider my answer for a minute, but I won't be able to make it on time. These workouts are cheaper than the private ones, but it's too stressful, thanks to my busy "to-do" list.

"Sorry, I'll pass this time. I'm so sorry for the late notice," I answer eventually and add a sad emoji.

It's half past two, and I prepare myself for Mia's daily call, trying to remember what I left her for lunch. There's some of Ilene's pasta and maybe some chicken. My phone rings and disturbs my thoughts. I take a deep breath.

Unfortunately, this isn't Mia.

It's the kind of call no mother is happy to receive.

2

TARA

I've been trying to make the most of my maternity leave since I promised Jason, the branch manager, I'd be back by April, but time passes so swiftly this morning. I had my roots done, and I have manicure and hair-straightening appointments set for next week. At my age, it's a must.

About a month ago I started practicing Pilates at Rylie's' new home studio. She moved to our neighborhood a few months ago, and she's unreasonably passionate about Pilates. Although she's nice and very professional, I won't be able to attend her workouts once I return to work, but Rylie says it's better than doing nothing.

As the deputy branch manager, I was expected to return to the bank ASAP, preferably ten days after giving birth to Emma. I prolonged it for five months. After all, she's my fourth and last child; therefore, this is also my last maternity leave. I know that once I get back to work, I'll be the last person leaving the branch each night, as usual.

I don't miss the long hours, but I do miss being out of the house. I enjoy the challenges, including helping businesses get the million-dollar loans they desperately need. Karen says that she wishes she had more time with her girls, but when she's home, she complains that it's too hard for her. I don't get it. The diaper-changing isn't very satisfying, I must admit, but it's easy compared to what I did at the bank.

I take Emma for a stroll in the neighborhood to get some air while Ethan sends me links all morning with options for the Easter holiday. Magnificent beaches, crystal-clear water, blue skies. He prefers last-minute holidays and suggested we all travel before I return to the bank, but he's crazy if he thinks we can enjoy a vacation with a four-and-a-half-month-old baby. I suggested we leave the baby with Juvi, our au pair. Maybe we can leave Mason, Ella, and Emily with her as well. I smile when I think about my mom's constant remarks: "Even on your maternity leave your au pair takes care of your baby? Who ever heard of such an arrangement?"

Our trip last year to Tuscany was sort of a birthday present. We left the kids with Juvi, and my mother was appalled. After all these years, she fails to accept that Juvi's a much better care-giver than Ethan.

That trip saved our marriage, coming after a stressful decade in which family life was a challenge we couldn't over-come together. We argued a lot, including about his lack of parenting, for example. He couldn't understand why I was upset about his nonstop trips with his stupid friends, trips for which I'd get only a day's notice. I tried to explain that being a parent means that you can't disappear like that again and again. Ethan said that I put too many limits on his freedom. *What parent has freedom?* I wanted to ask.

Each time we argue about this, Ethan promises to spend more time with the kids, and he even took Mason to a basket-ball game once or twice, though he mentions time and again what a sacrifice this is for him, being a football fan himself.

When we were younger, our worries were limited to choosing a restaurant for dinner. We could wake up and – just like that – decide to take a vacation. We didn't overthink anything and enjoyed ourselves. Every day was different, and we never knew where we'd end up at night.

Then came the kids, and everything changed in a heartbeat – but not for Ethan. We went from being a couple to a couple with one child, then two, and then three, and four. Ethan continued to live as he did before, and I became the responsible adult. One day he arrived with Juvi. Without asking me, he just brought her home, saying he had fixed everything. She's stayed with us ever since.

At first, it wasn't natural for me to have someone in my home, walking around, cooking, touching my things. But as time passed, I realized that for the first time since I became a mother, I had a true partner. I came home each day to a clean house and happy, clean kids. I got some of my freedom back and a lot more patience for Ethan. He bought himself peace and quiet when he hired Juvi. Looking back, it seemed it was the best surprise ever, and surprises are the thing he does best.

On Christmas, after dating for a couple years, we traveled to London for the weekend. All the streets were decorated with colorful lights, and it was freezing cold. Ethan booked us a ride on the London Eye for sunset, which should have made me very suspicious since he never books things in advance. We were crazy in love, though, and we were so happy together. I simply wasn't thinking clearly.

We took a black cab but still froze during the short walk. We went through the line, and within seconds we were inside the see-through capsule. Only when they closed the door did I notice that we were alone. The floor was covered with tall lit candles, and in the middle was a sign bearing the words "Marry Me." I was speechless. I looked around as the capsule went slowly up, and I saw all the buildings lit up beautifully in the night. It was amazing. Ethan knelt and opened a red velvet box, displaying a big diamond ring. It was as if a Hollywood director planned it all to the last detail.

"Will you marry me?" he said, as if following a romantic-comedy script.

"Yes!" I answered in a shaky voice. Ethan put the most impressive ring I have ever seen on my finger, and we kissed for a very long time. Only then did I notice the romantic music in the background. The lights went dark, so we could see the amazing view of the city. After taking off our coats, Ethan poured two glasses of the champagne he had ordered for us. He was prepared for everything.

When we arrived back at the hotel, I called Dad. He was happy for me, and so was Mom. I guess she thought that, at the age of thirty, I would never marry and considered me a lost cause. "I had four daughters when I was your age," she told me over and over again at every family gathering, like a broken record. Ethan was the perfect man in her eyes, although I believe she would have thanked anyone willing to rescue me from my status as a single woman.

While I push the stroller back home, I look at my hands and the diamond shining brightly in the late morning sun. Emma smiles back at me. She was another great surprise.

It all started on my forty-second birthday when Ethan made a reservation for the new fancy Italian restaurant, something that couldn't be done unless you knew someone who knew someone. And Ethan did. We met his friend Alex and his girl-friend, whose name I don't remember, but she was so boring and we never saw her again anyway. She kept complaining about everything. The location was too close to the bathroom, her meat was too dry, the room was too cold. I just wanted to stick the bread in her mouth so she would shut up. Poor Alex. It was completely not the evening I hoped it would be. I would have preferred going out with Karen and Adam, but Ethan said they bored him.

The only positive thing that came out of that horrible evening was the trip to Tuscany. Alex went on and on about how they enjoyed the time they spent there, and Ethan was so excited about it. The next day Ethan came back with two tickets to fly there for the weekend. It was sort of a surprise birthday trip, but the real surprise was finding out I was pregnant with Emma. Who thought I could get pregnant at forty-two?

Emma was an easygoing baby right from the start. At her age, Mason was so hard to handle, and Ella was always a bit hyperactive, wandering off the second I looked away. Lucky for me, Emma is a smaller version of Emily – quiet but determined.

It's unbelievable that I have four children. Four! I grew up with three sisters, and my mom stayed home with us, waiting every day for us to arrive home from school and allowing us to stay home whenever we felt slightly ill, even without fever. Growing up with her, daycare was foreign to us, and Mom thought it was the same as child neglecting – and maybe worse, like ready-cooked meals or having a babysitter. It's true that, thanks to her, I am a great cook. I can give her that. But she can never understand the way I raise my children.

What bugs me the most is her relationship with Ethan. She adores him as if he is the son she never had. If he compliments her once on something she cooks, she cooks it for him every time we come to dinner.

"He works so hard," she says – as if I don't.

My parents were together from the time my mom was fifteen till the day my dad died. It was a different time. You stuck together no matter what.

"You are your father's daughter," my mom used to say. "You look like him and you act like him." When I was younger, I thought it was a compliment. I know better now. In a way, she always envied our relationship.

When Dad came home from work – every day at the same

time – to me, he looked like James Bond in his dark suit, his black briefcase in his hand, a worn-out smile on his tired face. Over dinner, he would tell me about interest rates, currencies, and inflation, overwhelming me with his knowledge. I swallowed his every word while my sisters swallowed the ice cream he used to buy us on his way home. By the age of ten, I knew I would be a banker like him. He would have been so proud to see how I'd risen through the ranks at the bank. I know he would.

When I get back home with Emma, I see Ethan's car in the driveway. He prefers to leave for his car dealership after rush hour.

"It sounds like a blast," I hear his voice from the front yard. "You must get me in on it!" He always talks so loudly.

I enter the house with Emma's stroller, and she smiles at him. Ethan waves at me but continues his conversation using his new AirPods. He's wearing his usual outfit – black T-shirt and skinny black jeans. All his clothes are the same, as if it's his uniform. His black baseball hat covers his thin, dyed-black hair. Coloring his hair every month is his only routine other than smoking. Taking his car keys, Ethan waves at me as he leaves the house.

For the first time today, the house is quiet. Juvi takes Emma and sings a Filipino children's song to her as I flip slowly through the mail. When I get to the envelope from the law office, I tear it open impatiently and take out the letter. It was approved, and I sigh.

I put the letter on the table and smile. My mom will kill me.

3

RYLIE

In my Nike blue tights, matching crop top, and the new running shoes Noah bought me on one of his many business trips to London, I stand in front of the mirror. I'm getting ready for a run when he comes back from his office, and I feel it burning inside me – the desire to go outside into the evening air and feel my pulse rising, my muscles burning, the sweat. Moments of health and happiness. I try vigorously to fit these moments into my daily routine.

Even though I'm excited to get out of the house, I don't abandon Noah just like that. The boys are ready for bed after showers. A couple stories and they're done. Not too bad.

I know Danielle will come down for dinner soon, which means it's my time to get out of the house. She always wants something to eat as soon as I finish cleaning the kitchen after dinner. Always. As if it's beneath Her Highness to eat with her brothers – well, stepbrothers. I feel like her servant. God forbid I refuse her requests.

I hear her door opening. That's my cue. Let Noah handle his princess. I fix my ponytail and leave the house quietly so that the boys won't hear the door closing behind me. I sigh.

The weather's great for running. Not too cold and no rain. Just perfect.

While we were living in the village closer to my parents, I could run every day. Not only did it have more open fields than this neighborhood, but it was also easier for Mom to pop in and help us out. Noah used to join me, if he wasn't away somewhere trying to find investors for his start-up. It used to be our quality time, just the two of us.

Not anymore. Since we rented this house, no one can stay with the boys at night. Even when my mom comes to help us, Dad picks her up even before Noah arrives because Dad doesn't like driving late at night.

I run by Karen's and see her blond hair through her kitchen window. It's always so loud at her place. I can't understand how this quiet, gentle woman manages to live there. Although I only know her from the workouts she's joined, I do know that she works hard and has three girls and that besides her mother-in-law, nobody helps her. Tara told me that Karen's parents died one right after the other. Maybe that's why she's so quiet, hardly sharing anything about herself.

Tara works even harder, and I hardly saw her before her maternity leave. I only saw her husband, who parks his car on the pavement almost up to the entrance to our parking space. Some days it's impossible to walk through with the kids. Noah says that Ethan's not the kind of man you can talk to, so I tried asking Tara about it, but nothing changed. Noah says I should drop it.

A few weeks ago, I met Tara at Sammi's shop, and she gave me a recipe for spaghetti and meatballs. I cooked it several times, and the kids loved it. I was surprised to find out she cooks, given that she has her own au pair at home.

From the start, it was obvious that Noah would prefer to live next to his daughter at some point. His annoying, red-haired ex-wife, Sarah, lives in this suburb, where they used to live

together. Danielle grew up here, and it's her home. I do understand that. Noah only wants what's best for Danielle, and I
want what's best for him.

We moved here after Thomas was born, and I had no idea
being this close to Danielle would affect me so much. Danielle
stays with us more, and I have another child to take care of –
but it's more than that. She's disorganized, clumsy, and dirty.
Living in the same house with her – and especially sharing a
kitchen with her – is a nightmare. When she cooks something,
it's as if a bomb has exploded in there.

On top of all that, the only house we could find has only
three bedrooms, and it's a huge inconvenience that Aiden must
share his room with Thomas so that the princess can have her
own room. Every time Thomas cries at night, Aiden wakes up
as well. Have I already said that it's a nightmare? Why does she
need her own room for a couple nights a week and every
second weekend?

Noah promised that once he earns real money from selling
his company, we'll buy our own house – a bigger house with
five bedrooms and a nice studio for my Pilates, maybe even a
separate entrance for my studio and a separate toilet. I wish it
would happen already ... the sooner the better.

I don't fully understand what Noah develops in his
company (and by "company" I mean him and his friend). It's
some kind of firewall, I think, though I'm not completely sure.
They worked on it for years, and every few months I hear that
soon they'll have a life-changing meeting. Every business trip is
a crucial trip that can change it all. Surprisingly enough,
nothing ever happens. At least, it hasn't happened yet.

Tonight I hope to finish at least five miles. It's been a year
since Thomas was born, and I'm not back to my old self yet.
Noah says I look amazing, but I must admit that, next to Sarah,
all women look amazing. For her sake, I hope Danielle didn't
inherit her mom's body structure. Aiden already looks like a

small version of Noah. He's got Noah's curly hair, blue eyes, and his height; no one believes he's only three and a half. Thomas is too young to draw many comparisons, but you can see his resemblance to my father. Danielle is more like her mother – short and red-haired, though it's curly, like her father's. She's getting fuller each time I see her, and recently I saw her more than I want to.

"Does she help you when she's at your place?" Karen asked me during her last workout. I almost laughed. Help? From Danielle? Never. She interferes, screams, shouts, and gets in our way. Aiden knows better than to be around her when she starts. He just goes somewhere else. Thomas still smiles at her when she comes, even though she looks down at him with disgust. He'll learn.

"Not as much as you'd expect," I answer as politely as I can, but then I tell her everything.

I tell Karen how Noah lets Danielle do whatever she wants. How he won't marry me because of her. And how she treats me as if I'm the stepmother from hell. She's even rude to my parents. No matter how much I try, she's obnoxious.

"It's like living in a minefield," I say, "and what Danielle does best is spreading mines all over." I almost cry.

It's been a while since I opened up to someone like that. I miss my friends. I've hardly seen them since we moved here. I miss being able to tell my friends anything, things I can't even tell my mom – and definitely not Noah. Karen didn't share much, but I felt close to her.

"It's a rough age, I've heard," she says eventually. "Too bad. She seems like a nice girl."

"She's not," I say. Maybe Karen doesn't fully realize what I'm dealing with.

"If you find a sitter, please let me know. I really need some help in the afternoons." Karen stands up.

"Sure," I answer. She has an "almost" teenager in-house.

Why can't Mia help? My older sister took care of me when she was nine. Anyway, I don't know anyone, let alone other teenagers, except Danielle's friends, and I would never recommend them as babysitters.

I run in a "Sarah-free" street. I don't want to see her. Just the thought of her being so close gives me chills. I saw her with her boyfriend several times at Sammi's, and he actually looks very nice. But still, not seeing her is better. When we meet, I can feel her condescending look, and I know she would take Noah in a heartbeat if she could. Sometimes I wish she would get a job offer in Australia or some other faraway place, a place where she would take Danielle with her, of course.

My wristwatch shows I'm at eight miles. I wonder if Danielle is back in her room by now and whether Noah cleaned my kitchen after her. I enter the house with a hint of hope. The coast is clear.

I go upstairs, and her bedroom door is slightly open. Peeping inside, I see Danielle holding something before she puts it under her pillow. Is it a snack? I'm not sure. Danielle must have noticed me because she slams the door in my face.

I have a feeling she's hiding something.

4

KAREN

"Mia's teacher said she had no choice but to respond harshly to any act of violence," I tell Adam after the girls fall asleep and we have some time for ourselves. "She said Mia's suspended for an hour from the classroom. It's so embarrassing – and I'm on the PTA. I'm so ashamed."

"If it's just for an hour, it's not that bad. It's actually good that she knows how to defend herself. Do you know who the poor boy is? If someone needs to be embarrassed, it's him," Adam says with a smile.

"Good to know this mess pleases you, but violence isn't the solution to Mia's problem – and it seems to me that it's Mason, which is even more unpleasant. Tara hasn't called yet, so I'm not sure he has told her."

Adam smiles and leaves the room when Olivia calls for him again. *What's her problem with the blanket?* I really do not know how a five-year-old finds herself inside the duvet cover every time.

The phone call with the teacher was awkward. The last time Mia screamed at a girl from her class, the teacher sent me a message and asked us to talk to her. This time she pushed a boy who mocked her. I apologized to the teacher as if I had pushed the child myself.

Mia wouldn't tell me what happened, but I realized it's probably the same story with Mason again. He's been bullying her nonstop since the beginning of the year. It's not something I ever thought I would have to deal with, and I'm not sure how to talk about it with Tara. She's convinced Mason's an angel. She isn't willing to do anything about it, and I've tried several times in the past year.

"And by the way, I forgot to tell you that all my tests came back normal. Despite what your mother said, I'm not anemic, and I don't have an iron insufficiency," I tell Adam after he returns – for the eighth time – from Olivia's room. Ilene said that because I'm picky about what I eat, I lack vitamins, and that's why I'm tired and have no energy to do the house chores. I explained that house chores are not a matter of energy but of priorities. It didn't help.

"That's great," Adam says, unbuttoning the white shirt he wore for a court hearing.

"Totally. But it doesn't explain why I'm so tired all the time." I even thought I was pregnant again, so I checked that as well. Twice. It was negative, thank God. I can hardly get along with the three I have now.

This tiredness started to really worry me when I stayed at the office to take care of a malfunction in one of the sites one night after my team left for the day. During the update, I rested my head on my desk – just for a second, I thought. The next thing I knew, my phone was ringing and I woke up in a panic. It was Adam, worried because it was nine o'clock and I hadn't come home. I don't know how long I slept exactly, but my neck was stiff. The whole thing was out of character for me since I usually have a hard time falling asleep in my own bed.

After this strange incident, I asked for all the blood tests possible, explaining to the doctor that I feel that something's wrong with me and that this fatigue isn't typical for me. He said it's clear that a mother of three children ("three girls," I corrected him) who's working full-time would be tired.

"You complain for years that something's bothering you, but all the tests come back normal. Maybe you should take it easy?" Adam dares to offer, "You're not as young as you were when we met."

"Don't go there," I say, and he smiles.

Adam takes off his eyeglasses, cleaning them with his T-shirt. His hair's no longer as well-groomed as it was at the beginning of the day, and his bristled face looks as if he hasn't shaved for a week. He looks exhausted. As a junior partner in a law firm, he works a lot and gets less than he deserves – in my opinion, at least. Adam never complains, but I do, mostly because he's not present enough to really help around the house. Even though I also work full-time, for some reason, all afternoon parenting chores are on me.

When we started dating, I discovered Adam is sensitive, quiet, and loving. The only drawback to dating him was his relationship with his mother. At first, I thought it was cute and wonderful to find a man who loves his mother as much as I loved mine. Ilene called him every night before bed, and every weekend she sent containers of food to our small student apartment. Every Friday he visited them, and I joined the tradition that remains to this day.

With the wedding and the children that followed, we wanted to raise our kids in a community farther away from the loud, crowded city. We wanted a different atmosphere, but still close enough to all we need. This small neighborhood was exactly what we were looking for: small townhouses with red-tiled roofs and manicured gardens, community gardens and parks on every corner, and a local grocery. Everyone knows everyone. Every Friday afternoon the community center shows a kid's movie for free, and there are community events every holiday. We even go hiking together every spring and plant trees every fall. I organized it, actually, and it became a new, lovely tradition.

Another bonus we received was neighbors who became good friends. Mason, Tara's son, has been in school with Mia since kindergarten. That's how we met them. Later her three daughters were born and our two daughters. We couldn't have planned our pregnancies so close even if we tried. The bigger ones never bonded – maybe because he's a boy – but the rest get along just wonderful. Olivia and Ella are in the same kindergarten, and it will be very comfortable if they start first grade together.

Until a few months ago, my good friend Daria lived next door, but they left because of a job offer in Boston. In their place, Rylie and Noah rented the house. Rylie's very passionate about and deeply immersed in the recent health obsession (that has become a kind of modern-day epidemic, if you ask me). Nevertheless, I've started practicing Pilates at her studio occasionally. That's what makes this neighborhood so convenient. Everything's so close.

"If you're already in bed, maybe I'll have a quick shower and join you for some quality time?" Adam says, gently shoving the blanket that covers me as he sits next to me.

I look at him with a look that goes from "won't happen now" to "what the heck do you think?"

"The girls are asleep," he pleads before I can even say anything.

"Not today. I'm dead tired."

"You're always tired." He stands up in one sharp movement, and I see the anger in his eyes.

"What can I do about it? I'm trying my best, you know."

"We can't go on like this!" Adam walks inside our bathroom and closes the door behind him.

I look at the closed door, not understanding where all these emotions have come from. Doesn't he see that I'm tired and weak? Doesn't he understand that I'm going through something? Doesn't he live with me in the same house? It's like he doesn't listen to what I'm saying.

It's so disappointing to realize that no matter what I do – taking care of the girls (carpools, homework, and wiping the bottoms of their small friends), full-time management of a team of employees (one who separated from his boyfriend, Anna just stopped taking her antidepressants, and one that seems to forget I'm in charge), going to PTA meetings (buying gifts for teachers' day, arranging parents' duties, and collecting the fees), active in the neighborhood committee (organizing lectures and planting, plus heading the cleaning committee), taking care of the house (replacing light bulbs, schedule with the gardner, ordering the plumber) – at the end of another exhausting day, I'm judged by only one thing: how frequently I have sex with my husband.

When Adam comes out of the bathroom, he walks to his side of the bed, picks up his pillow, and says, "We can't go on like this." Then he takes his blanket and leaves the room.

5
_____

TARA

"I don't understand what it was good for," Mom says angrily as I answer her call.

"What are you talking about?" I know exactly what she's talking about, but I prefer to be safe and avoid entering into an unnecessary confrontation.

"Your father's will! Why was it so urgent to confirm it now in court? Why?" Mom screams. In this case, the post office was extra efficient.

"How long can we drag this on? It's just a little bureaucracy we need to handle. Don't make it more than it is," I try.

"The fact that Dad left you his share of the house – and not your sisters – does not mean you have to wave it in their faces."

"Who's waving? It's mine. It doesn't matter if you validate the will or not. Besides, it doesn't change anything. You live there, right? I'm not asking you to pay rent. It's just formalities, that's all."

"It's petty, that's what it is. And you could give up your part. You could sign that you're giving it up. Right?"

"Dad wanted it this way. It wasn't my decision. And there's no reason I should give up my part." I feel my temperature rising, and I almost lose my patience. "Mom, I'm in the middle of cooking for the weekend. Let's talk about it when you come in the evening, okay?"

"We have nothing to talk about," she says angrily, and the call breaks off.

I take a deep breath and fix my hair behind my ear. I waited many years before I even went to a lawyer to handle Dad's will, validating the will first. I knew it would make Mom angry, so I decided to do it gradually.

When Dad told me he wanted to give me the house, I understood why. He didn't have to say anything. My little sister isn't a reliable adult. Even now, at thirty-five, she still spends half her time in India practicing Yoga. It's unclear what she's looking for there, but it is clear that she hasn't found it yet. My older sisters don't understand anything about anything. Both are married to men who manage them financially, and they prefer it that way.

I sit down next to the kitchen island and prepare a list of everything I want to cook for dinner. When Mom tastes something I cook, the stress of it burns inside me. She's never satisfied, saying things like, "I usually put lemon in it," and "I would broil it, not fry it." But these aren't the only things she criticizes. She has strong opinions about everything I do. "A mother needs to raise her kids herself," she always tells me.

Since I was a girl, I knew what I wanted to do when I grew up. I wanted to be like Dad, which annoyed Mom even more. My two older sisters fulfilled all her aspirations by staying home and raising their children. I'm the rebel. I went to university, got married late, and have a career as a deputy branch manager. For her, I'm the failure. Lucky for me, Dad didn't agree with her. He believed in me and trusted me. He knew Mother would be in good hands.

I wash the green beans I want to add to the dish, just like Grandma's recipe. As a child, I would sit with her in the kitchen and help her cut vegetables. If Mom saw me using a frozen mix, she would have something to say about it, that's for sure. She doesn't understand that I work hard at the bank and I want to cut some corners when I can. It's my right to choose where to invest my energies.

The house is still relatively quiet. Juvi left with Emma to bring back the children from school, and Ethan hasn't returned yet ... and maybe that's better.

This morning Ethan informed me that he was going sailing spontaneously with some friends, including Alex, who always walks around with a blue Uniqlo coat. These are the moments I just want to scream. When he spends time with his friends, it usually ends up badly. His habit of disappearing on Fridays gets on my nerves.

"Come back in time to pick them up from school. I have to cook," I said, holding Emma, who follows me everywhere like a puppy. Emily wore her most beautiful white dress this morning, and I know that this dress will return in a completely different color at the end of the day.

"Jovita can take them. What am I paying her for?" he said, taking a clean towel.

Ooh ... I hate this answer, as if by hiring Juvi he got a "get out of jail free" card from parenting tasks. And when I think about it, is *he* paying? I earn more than him most months.

"Juvi's taking care of Emma. You can take them once. It won't kill you, you know."

"Come on. Leave me alone already!"

For a moment, I wanted to ask him if he'd like to join Emily in daycare. Instead, I said, "And don't commit to anything with your friends."

"What can I commit to?" he asked innocently, as if I was stupid.

"I don't know, but I know you. You jump at any offer in a heartbeat." I stood next to him as Emma sucked on the necklace I inherited from Grandma. Emily pulled my shirt behind me.

"You always complain about this deal, but you'll see that it's going to make us tons of money. It's going to be a great deal. If it succeeds, I'll get you another Jovita." He looked all over for his favorite blue baseball cap.

"I don't need another Juvi. All I need is peace. No more adventures."

"Relax. This is the deal of a lifetime. Do you know how many people want to join the project? I'm lucky Alex asked me to join." As always, he raised his voice and didn't even notice. He put on his hat and walked down the stairs.

"Really lucky," I said, following him downstairs with Emma, who was laughing out loud and enjoying herself. Emily was still behind me, but she had given up and released my unfortunate shirt.

"You have no faith," Ethan said. I wanted to strangle him with his blue hat.

"I have faith in facts. In reality. Something you have a problem understanding, apparently," I said as anger filled me.

"Leave me alone!" He took his car keys and left.

That's how every conversation ends with him lately. He goes and leaves me frustrated. All the positive feelings I had for him last night as we sat outside, drinking wine and talking, disappeared completely. As soon as I don't agree with him, he becomes another person.

It's amazing how easy it is to forget everything: The laughs and love. All we had between us in our early years together. Sometimes I really need to remind myself why I stay with him at all. Are a few moments of grace worth all the pain?

"A woman must support her husband." Mom's words go through my head. Talking to her is like going back in time, to a period when women were submissive and men ran the world. If she happens to ask me what I'm doing, she expects to hear me tell her what I cooked for lunch. If I tell her I'm taking care of business customers worth millions, she just pulls her shoulders and says something like, "I'd rather you take care of your children."

I hope the cruise doesn't lead us to another adventure or, as Ethan calls it, another "once in a lifetime opportunity."

I imagine – jokingly, of course – how I would react if I were to be notified that Ethan was swept out to sea. I'm smiling. Well, maybe it wouldn't be so bad.

6

RYLIE

"Why don't you leave your phone and buckle up already?" I ask Danielle as I put Thomas in his car seat.

"Leave me alone," she growls, taking another picture for her Instagram status ("on the way to dinner") and delaying us all.

I give up and decide to leave her in Noah's care. It's so upsetting to be late for my parents because of her nonsense. Last time we were almost an hour late because she waited for the particular shirt she wanted to wear to get out of the dryer – just a complete lack of consideration.

"Danielle, dear, put on your seat belt please. We're late," Noah smiles.

"Ahh," she replies.

I hear a click, and we finally pull out of our drive and head to my parents.

"My baby!" Mommy opens the door, and I extend the hug as long as possible, letting it calm me down a bit. Aiden and Thomas happily enter and get warm hugs as well before running to Dad where he sits on his couch, watching TV. They climb up and curl up next to him.

"Hi, Daddy," I say and go straight into the kitchen, putting the bag with all my mom's containers on the countertop. Danielle slowly drags herself into the house like a wounded turtle and comes in last without saying hello.

"Hello, Danielle, how are you?" Mom smiles at her like she does every time they meet, trying to get some attention from Danielle.

"Fine," Danielle answers without looking up from the screen as she throws herself onto the sofa. Just peachy.

I give Mommy a desperate look of *What can I do?* and she smiles and whispers to me, "Patience."

The meal goes relatively well. Thomas, as always, steals everyone's attention, smiling sweetly and throwing his food everywhere. Danielle just frowns and eats nothing but rice. I already know that when we get back home, she'll be hungry, and I'll have to cook something for her. As usual. And even then, she'll find something to complain about.

"She's unbearable. I can't do it anymore," I whisper to Mommy as I help her clean the kitchen after dinner.

Noah sits in the living room and talks to my dad about raising money for his start-up. Dad seems quite pleased with the progress. At least in that aspect, he's calm. Dad never talks to me about the fact that we aren't married, but I know from Mommy that it bothers him.

"What choice do you have, love? You must get along with her. She's his daughter." Mommy fills a container with rice. "Take it for her."

"She behaves terribly. She's rude and does whatever she wants regardless of who's around. Today at noon I wanted Thomas to sleep, and she purposely played music loud enough to disturb him. He hardly slept, and you see how tired he is now." I fill another container with Mom's chicken cutlets for tomorrow.

"She'll grow out of it. It's a challenging age." Mommy hugs me, which frees the tears I held inside all evening.

"Mommy, it's been like this for years – even when she was younger – and it's only getting worse. They spoil her."

I try to stop the tears but can't. My body shakes, and the frustration is unbearable. I don't want Danielle to see me cry, so I wipe my face with a paper towel.

"My baby, you have to understand that things aren't easy for her." Mommy kisses me gently on the cheek, and I notice new wrinkles at the sides of her eyes.

"What's not easy? She has everything she wants!" My whisper almost becomes a shout.

"The divorce was difficult for her, love, and it's easier for her to blame you for it instead of her parents," Mommy says quietly, stroking my face gently. With her finger, she collects another tear that slipped out.

"Is it my fault that her mother treated Noah so bad that he left her?"

"No, love. Of course not. But you know what happened. She doesn't," Mommy says quietly.

Sometimes I grow a little tired of her protecting Danielle. She is *my* mother, and she should be on *my* side. "Well, never mind. This girl is a lost cause. We have to go now."

"Everything will be fine, love." Mom puts all the containers, including the rice, in a bag. She hugs me, and we return to the living room together. Noah gets the hint and lifts sleeping Thomas from the sofa.

"Good night, Rachel," Noah says, and Mommy kisses Thomas's head.

"Good night, drive carefully." Mommy walks with us outside, and Aiden walks by me, rubbing his tired eyes. "Good night, Danielle," she tells the little monster.

Danielle goes the extra mile and answers, "Bye," as she follows us and gets into the car, this time without protest. Maybe it's a kind of progress. I watch her sitting in the back seat with her two stepbrothers. Aiden looks at her admirably, and I hope that one day she'll treat him better. Truthfully, some kind of attention from her side would be nice.

We park and try to take the sleeping kids to bed without waking them, each of us holding a sleeping angel. Tara and Ethan stand at the entrance to their house, saying goodbye to their family with hugs and kisses.

Tara wears a dress that really complements her body. She always dresses so elegantly for work. Every outfit she wears probably costs what I earn in a month, not to mention her jewelry, which is worth probably more than our monthly rent.

Even now she's wearing a necklace made of large blue beads. I must ask her where it's from. They smile and wave at us as they return home together.

Everything looks so simple for them. No redhead divorcee. No teenage girl from hell. A husband, a wife, and kids. A normal, uncomplicated family. Their only concern is where to take their next vacation and whether to take the Filipino au pair with them.

What a dreamy life Tara has.

7

KAREN

All the way home from school Olivia doesn't stop talking. She complains about the amount of homework she has and about the new seating arrangement in class that put her next to a girl she hates. I promise to talk to her teacher. Again. I try to concentrate on her stories about that girl, but I feel like I'm sleepwalking. I have a workout tonight at Rylie's studio, and I have no idea how to stay awake until then.

We come home, and Mia welcomes me in tears accompanied by nonstop screaming. I can understand a word or two: *Mason. Awful. Teacher.*

"Mia, stop talking for one second." I put my bag down on the table.

"Mason told me I was ugly and fat, so I yelled at him and now the teacher's mad at me because of him. I swear I didn't push him!"

"Okay. That's good. We'll explain to her what happened." I'm relieved that this time it didn't end in violence. This is already some progress.

"It's too late. She hates me!" Mia runs to the living room and lies down on the couch, crying. Lucky me, the maid was here earlier today, and the couch is laundry-free. "I want to move to another class! I can't stand being there anymore!"

"You don't need to transfer to another class. The school year's almost over."

"Next year I don't want to be in this class either!" Mia continues to scream and cry. "And tell Tara her son's annoying and I hate him!"

"All right, all right. Stop crying. I'll talk to your teacher."

The little ones relax in front of the screen, and I lie down next to them on the couch. Mason has been bothering Mia for a while, and even before the last encounter with him, I tried to talk to Tara about the problems between the kids. At first, Tara said it was just his desire to get Mia's attention.

Then we spoke again, and I asked her to talk to him. After all, they're our neighbors and the kids have known each other since they were two. It's unclear why they can't get along, and I just hope it doesn't affect my friendship with Tara. She's my only friend, and I hardly have time to talk to her.

When Daria lived here, we were very close. She worked from home and was always available to listen to me. I told her everything – she was like the sister I never had. Our kids were the same age too, so we literally raised them together. Since she moved, it's not the same, and I'm really lonely.

I look at Mia lying next to me. Her show is on, but she's staring at her phone, her eyes still red from crying. She's going through a difficult time, and I'm already in despair. I don't know how to help her anymore. She seems to be angry with me for being friends with Tara, as if I'm doing something against her, as if I'm cheating on her. At her age, she still cannot understand that we're old enough to separate being a parent from being a friend.

When the children were younger, Tara and I carpooled together – I mean, Juvi and I carpooled since Tara was barely there. To my knowledge, she hadn't seen the children's teacher all year long. Tara is either working or vacationing – preferably abroad and as far away as possible. Almost every vacation is abroad, and they also manage to travel without the children because they have Juvi. I don't remember when Adam and I went without the girls for a couple's vacation. Ilene, Adam's mother, probably remembers.

"Mom, I'm hungry." I open my eyes and see Olivia standing in front of me. I must have fallen asleep.

"I'm up," I say but don't move. Amelia curls up next to Mia, and Olivia sits back on the couch.

What can I do about this fatigue? It's getting worse and worse, and I recently noticed that my right hand is weak. In Pilates, my right foot seems weaker than my left. Rylie says we're not symmetrical, that there's always a strong side and a weak side, and that I should come more and strengthen my right side. Today I feel I have no strong side at all.

I get up and go to the kitchen to prepare omelets. The girls know not to expect more for dinner in the middle of the week when Adam isn't home, and I can ruin that too. Mia likes to remind me how I burned an omelet I prepared for her friend.

My body feels like it's burdened with weights as I clear the table of all Adam's nonsense. He keeps buying gadgets for his bicycles and has now arranged for himself a charger to recharge his cell phone while riding.

But the most annoying aspect of this expensive hobby is that he wakes up at five every Saturday morning to ride with his friends. Sometimes he wakes Amelia, and I must start entertaining her that early – on a Saturday! The only advantage is that his beer belly is gone.

I hear the front door opening and know that Adam's home. Olivia and Amelia run to him with enthusiasm reserved only for fathers, apparently.

"I'm going upstairs for a rest. Can you finish here?" I don't wait for an answer and start upstairs to the bedroom. Before I close the door, I shout, "And they haven't showered yet!"

No. There will be no sex today either. And if he has any complaints, he's welcome to submit them as he does in his office –in triplicate.

8

TARA

"Why do you have to tell the whole world about the investment you made with Alex?" I ask Ethan immediately after the door closes on the last guest to leave after another family dinner.

"What's the problem? Maybe your sister wants to join in too. I think there are some apartments left." Ethan sits down and sips beer from the bottle he left on the kitchen island. Meanwhile, Juvi collects the dishes, and I put the leftovers in the fridge. My sister doesn't really need this investment. She should keep the money she inherited from Dad in a safer place. I'll talk to her about it tomorrow before her enthusiastic husband goes along with Ethan's nonsense.

"Stop dragging more people with you. You have no idea what's going to happen. Something about this guy Alex doesn't seem right to me." I close the refrigerator door and look at Ethan. He sits there drinking his beer, watching me and Juvi organize the kitchen as if he's a guest in this house.

"Dragging? Who's dragging? You're just being hysterical." Ethan gets up to go upstairs.

"What about the documents? Did you take them from Alex's lawyer yesterday?" I finally remember to ask.

"He postponed the meeting for next week," he says and closes the door behind him.

"I have to clean here," Juvi says with a smile.

I wipe my hands and pour myself a glass of red wine, then go outside to the balcony and light a cigarette. I don't usually smoke, but I need to relax, and I need an excuse to stay downstairs for a while. The kids are already in bed, and it's Saturday. Mason goes to bed whenever he wants.

Ethan always forgets the crappy things he does and says. He has a negative learning curve, never learning from his mistakes. The first adventure started with something he presented as an attractive offer to buy an apartment as an investment. At the time I thought it was a good idea financially. We were a young couple with a child, and it seemed wise to invest our savings in real estate. Prices were low, and everyone said it was a wise decision. I had just started working at the bank, and Ethan was still an employee at the car dealership. I thought it would be a good investment for the future.

Ethan found a neglected small apartment in a bad neighborhood – or, as Ethan called it, "an area with potential." We renovated the apartment and rented it out. At the beginning it was great, and the rent slowly paid back our loans.

I liked the fact that Ethan took the initiative and tried to improve us financially. In those years I thought he was a kind of entrepreneur. I loved his adventurous nature and his courage, as well as his ability to see beyond what we had.

Ethan forgot to point out one small detail with the deal though: our tenant was an active member in a crime organization. One evening, the police called to report that the apartment had been burned and requested that we arrive at the station.

When the investigation was over, Ethan called me at the bank to tell me that it was determined that the cause of the fire was – thankfully – a short circuit and not arson.

"Call the insurance company," I said.

"There isn't any insurance."

I didn't understand what he was saying; that didn't make sense. A client approached my desk as I asked, quietly, "What do you mean?" My team manager stood behind me.

"I forgot to sign one stupid document they requested and the insurance isn't valid," he said indifferently.

"I don't understand. You're telling me that the apartment isn't insured?" I tried not to scream as the bank was filled with people.

"Everything will be fine. We'll take a loan and renovate again. What are you worried about?" His apathy became a complete lack of awareness, and it was then I started to realize he had a problem. Those days I wasn't earning the salary I'm earning today, and Ethan earned even less than I did, which didn't stop him from living far beyond our earnings. He was already into expensive watches.

"Just wait." I realized that I should find another place to have this conversation. I got up and went to the staff bathroom, closing the door behind me so they wouldn't hear me scream. I completely lost it.

"I'm working my butt off to pay all those loans! Who will give us another loan?"

"Stop the hysteria and the drama," Ethan said in his usual way. I'm "hysterical," and he's a "visionary." This has always been his motto.

"You're just awful!" I shouted and hung up. My hands trembled so badly that I almost dropped the phone into the toilet.

It took several years and a lot of hard work to overcome this crisis. Ethan slept great through it all while stress kept me awake for so many nights. I would lie in bed and think about how many extra hours I would have to work to repay the loans. I didn't even want to think about what Dad would say about

Ethan's stupid adventures. We were lucky I got promoted to deputy manager at the branch and earned enough to repay everything.

I must admit that Ethan's car dealership has succeeded beyond my anticipation. He manages to convince people to buy a car they don't need at a price they can hardly afford. At least he's found his place and has an excuse for his business trips to Germany and Italy. The problem with his job is the people he meets. He doesn't understand that not every person who can buy a Mercedes knows something about business.

So now he's embarking on a new adventure, this time with that rude Alex – a luxury seafront apartment only a five-minute drive from our burnt apartment. This time, I made sure he checked all the legal details, asking him a million times. He claims that his lawyer showed him all the documents and that it's legit. He swore to me that he signed the contract and will receive the signed documents this week. That was the only reason I allowed him to take our savings and invest them in this project.

And here we go again. He transferred our money and received nothing in writing. What an idiot. I don't know who this trustee is that Alex has chosen, and I only hope he's decent. Alex, on the other hand, doesn't seem like a decent person.

Every time I ask Ethan where the documents are, he says, "I trust him. I've known Alex for years – he won't screw me."

I hope he's right this time.

Ethan says I'm hysterical, but every day I meet business owners who weren't paid by a customer, and who now have trouble paying their suppliers. Every day I hear this story over and over again. As if he hasn't heard these stories from me, Ethan believes every person he sees only because he invited him for a beer. I ask him to consult with Adam, Karen's husband. He's a real estate lawyer.

"Tara, opportunities don't happen. You create them," he always says.

What's worse than having a jerk for a husband is having a husband who doesn't realize he's a jerk.

9

RYLIE

"I'm going for a run now, babe. Can you come down to be with the kids?" I shout to Noah as I tie my running shoes.

"I'm coming." He comes down with his little black bag that he just finished unpacking after another short trip to Berlin. Maybe this time that bag will spend a little more time in the closet. I hope.

"Bye, babe." I kiss him gently on the lips and see Danielle's face curve in disgust. I'm smiling. *Yes, Danielle, that's the situation now. Deal with it!*

She lies on the couch, concentrating on her phone that never stops beeping from all the messages she receives. Aiden plays with his PAW Patrol cars on the mat, apparently in another desperate attempt to get closer to her.

I get out of the house and run toward the scant fields that surround the neighborhood. Each year there are fewer and fewer of them. I need some time to myself, especially since Danielle draws all my energy when she stays at our place. How long can I force myself to be nice to her? The weekends with her are getting longer – and so are my runs.

I cross the road and enter the dry, yellow fields. Although

the kids will want to eat soon, I choose the longer route that surrounds the whole neighborhood. The less time I have with Danielle, the better it is for everyone.

If Noah wasn't so scared of her reactions, we probably would have gotten married already. Because of that – and only that – my parents don't have this closure yet.

"When will we dance at your wedding?" Mommy asks every now and then, particularly before family events, perhaps hoping that this time she'll be able to tell everyone that I'm finally getting married. I know that it's even more important for Dad, but he doesn't say anything. He always lets Mommy manage everything related to me and my sisters, as if he shouldn't deal with "women's issues."

"Very soon, I hope," I tell her and truly hope that one day it will come. I never thought I would have two children and zero weddings.

I met Noah while I was working as an instructor in a gym where Noah was training at the time. He was in one of my group workouts.

"We're old men – have some mercy on us," one of the guys whined. "Do you want us to have a heart attack?"

"You seem fine to me," I replied indifferently, not intending to change the training I had planned for them.

"On the inside, I'm a complete wreck," Noah replied, gasping, as his curls jumped up and down with him. "I'm used to being in the office all day, not keeping up with young girls."

I blushed but ignored his comment. I was used to men's disgusting comments, ranging from, "Check out my abs" to "Do you do individual workouts as well?"

Remarks like Noah's were relatively flattering, but it was his warm smile that caught my attention as it blended superbly with his dimples. His childish look made me think he was younger than he really was. During the push-ups, I moved as if by accident and saw that he had no ring on his finger. I hid a small smile I knew he couldn't see. At the end of the workout, I ignored his attempt to make eye contact, but I was glad he tried.

After a few inquiries, I knew he usually went to the gym cafe after the workout, so I made sure to sit alone at the first table, ensuring he couldn't miss me.

"May I join you?" Noah stood with his tray next to me and smiled the smile that he probably knew no woman could resist.

"Sure," I replied, trying not to sound enthusiastic, but my heart was racing like crazy.

"I'm Noah." He introduced himself and sat down, but I already knew his name.

"Hi, Noah. You're still alive, I see."

"Hardly." He looked me straight in the eye and smiled, his dimples standing out even more.

I examined his tray: salad, chicken breast, and rice. He clearly cared about what he was eating. That was a good start.

"How long have you worked here?" he asked, drinking his protein shake.

"A few months, but I recently gave them notice," I replied with a smile. I was eager to go on the trip I'd fantasized about for years.

"Good for you," Noah smiled, trying to cut the chicken breast that lay on the plate next to the rice. "Any interesting plans?"

"A six-month trip to Australia."

"Nice. My wife traveled there for a few months and had a great time," Noah said, and I felt all the air whoosh out of my lungs. "I've always dreamed of going on a caravan trip through New Zealand."

"Good to know," I said, referring mainly to the information about his wife's existence. I couldn't care less whether his wife enjoyed her trip or not. "Well, Noah, it was nice to meet you." I got up and took my tray, which was almost full. I'd completely lost my appetite.

"My pleasure," I heard him say, but I didn't bother to turn around. I left the cafe and went to my locker, disappointed that I let myself get carried away with thoughts that I'd met the love of my life. I felt so stupid.

After returning from Australia, I studied health and fitness for two years. One day, out of the blue, Noah sent me a text message.

"Hello to the toughest instructor in the gym. It's Noah, the one who almost died of a heart attack because of you, remember? Is there any chance you're free for coffee? Or tea?" He wrote as if we'd just seen each other yesterday.

"Does your wife allow you to drink coffee with someone who almost killed you?" I answered sarcastically, wondering if I should block his number.

"I didn't ask her because soon she won't be my wife anymore," he texted back instantly.

An uncontrollable, huge smile spread on my face, and I literally jumped up and down with excitement. I didn't even care how he got my number.

"If that's the case, then there's something to talk about," I wrote to him after a few minutes so that he wouldn't think I was too enthusiastic.

From the moment we had that coffee, it all happened very fast, and within a few months we moved in together. At first, I thought that he would propose to me in a matter of months. As I got to know Danielle and his relationship with her, I realized that it wouldn't happen so soon. At the age of twenty-five, I had Aiden, followed by Thomas, and not a ring in sight yet.

Noah constantly says he sees no point in remarrying as it won't change our relationship. He says his divorce was very traumatic. None of that is true. A wedding will send a clear message to Danielle that I'm here to stay and not going anywhere, no matter what drama she pulls. She'll understand that I've won.

I come home and pass through her room, wishing I had a room like that growing up. I shared mine with both my sisters. Danielle's is large with an adjustable double bed and a big smart TV – even bigger than the one we have in our room. I told Noah it really didn't make sense to pamper her like that, but he insisted.

Her door is open, and loud music fills the house. She's filming herself again with her new iPhone. It would be nice if she could find a silent activity sometimes.

"Do you have any homework?" I ask calmly, trying to look interested.

"Don't you have your own kids to bother?" she answers.

"We promised your mother that you would do your home-work when you stay with us." Actually, it was Noah who promised, and he left me to deal with it since he doesn't want to confront her.

"Don't tell me what to do, and don't even talk about my mother!" she shouts, and I feel her hatred in every word. The door slams, ending another typical conversation with Danielle.

"You saw how she behaved?" I ask Noah as I go downstairs after a quick shower. He sits in the living room with Thomas and Aiden and says nothing. "It's unbearable," I continue, mostly because I feel like I can't keep quiet. "You have to do something about it."

"She's a teenager – that's how they react," Noah says, bouncing Thomas on his knees. Thomas's curls hover around him like rays of sun in Aiden's paintings, and his laughs fill the house with joy.

"It's not an excuse. Other people live in this house, and they can't live with this behavior. I used to be a teenage girl too, and I never talked to anyone like that." I sit down at the table and take an apple from the clay bowl.

Almost all my conversations with Danielle end with a door slam. I ask her to clear her dishes to the sink; door slam. I ask her to turn down the music so that Thomas can rest; door slam. Noah always acts so gently with her, as if afraid that if he says something, she won't come to us anymore.

Noah puts Thomas back on the sofa next to Aiden and stands behind me, his long, strong arms surrounding me, and I feel like a little girl myself for a moment.

"You've got to take care of her," I tell him again, but this time not in anger. "I saw she also left a plate with leftover chocolate in her room. It's not healthy for her to eat all those sweets all the time, and it's also dirty and brings cockroaches. Really disgusting."

"I'll talk to her. I promise," Noah says softly and kisses me on the neck, his stubble tickling me.

Danielle used to be a cute girl with red, curly hair like her mother's. Now she's doing all kinds of nonsense to her hair. She flat irons it every few days, and she wants to have a permanent straightening. She's too young for this, but I know that eventually one of her parents will give in and agree. It was the same with the iPhone, and it was the same when she asked to color her hair blue.

As with many other things, they think that if they do what she wants, they're good parents, like the story with the sweets. We limit the amount of candy the boys can have per day, and if possible, I prefer they not have it every day. But Danielle can't be restricted. Noah lets her eat whatever she wants.

Noah constantly says that one day Danielle will accept my presence in her life. A few years have passed, and it hasn't happened. Next year I'll be thirty and officially still single. I've almost given up, but I won't.

I won't let these two redheads destroy my family.

10

KAREN

I stand in the conference room on the highest heels I can wear and smile with satisfaction. Despite the silence around me, in my mind, I hear wild applause. My presentation is excellent, and I summarize it in a slide describing everything we were able to accomplish in the new version of the software being released tonight. We even managed to fix some bugs that we planned to fix in the next version.

"Well done, Karen – and your hardworking team, of course." Will smiles contentedly as I'm sure he silently counts the money it will bring to the company.

Due to the release of the new version, I have to stay late at work, but I had planned for it to be one of the longest days of my week. Ilene and Jacob will stay with the girls until Adam returns.

It's a stressful day because I never know how and when it will end. It might be a perfect release, or the system might fail the second we update the version. Everyone's stressed-out around me, tired of working long hours around the clock. Despite all the stress, it's still easier for me to spend the afternoon here than at home with the girls – not that I'll admit it to anyone. If asked, I always complain that I'm not home as much I'd hoped. That's what moms are supposed to say, isn't it?

Ilene always says she doesn't understand what I have to complain about with three lovely, well-behaved girls – at least, that's how they behave with their grandma. They're scared of her because if she gets offended, she makes a scene as if she's a teenager herself. Adam obeys her too and makes sure to please her all the time, but the girls don't act like that with me, especially Mia. She argues about everything.

I head back to my desk as my team orders take-away from a Chinese restaurant. I eat the leftovers from Friday that I brought from home. Sometimes I feel guilty that I enjoy these long hours once a week, but then I remind myself that my presence in the office is important because it sets a personal example for my team. However, they have no children, and it's not the same. Anna is single, Ray lives with his boyfriend, and Dave is married but doesn't have any children. I don't think they understand the full ramifications when I stay late like I am today.

This doesn't mean that I'm not having fun with the girls. I love being with them on the weekends, with Adam, going on family trips, or just having a barbeque in the garden – but not all day every day. I eventually lose my patience and miss talking to another adult.

Last Friday, Adam wanted some time just for the two of us. We've both been busy at work recently, and we hardly spend time together without the girls. Ilene agreed, the girls stayed over at their house, and we went to a movie – not a movie about princesses or fairies, but an action movie like Adam loves. I wore a blue silk blouse, tailored black trousers, and my black high heels, even going so far as to put on some makeup. I really made an effort as I usually don't look like that during the weekends. I was in the mood for a romantic date.

We went to a cafe before the movie, and Adam asked me

what I wanted to do on my fortieth birthday. I had no ideas. It still seems so distant to me. Adam suggested we do something with friends, and I said I'd look at the options and prices, thinking it might be too expensive.

As we entered the cinema and the lights went out, I felt fatigue overtaking me. I closed my eyes – just for a second during the trailers – trying to think who I can invite to my birthday, now that Daria has moved away. Maybe Tara?

Adam says I fell asleep before the movie even started and that people looked at me, amused. The whole story is so embarrassing. I think about it now, and my face turns red. It never happened to me before. Even during my pregnancies, this didn't happen.

And, of course, Adam expected that after the movie we would continue the evening. He went in for a shower, and I was supposed to wait for him in bed, which I did. I even switched to a sexy black baby doll that we bought on our honeymoon.

Adam said he found me sleeping, curled up in my blanket, and couldn't wake me up, which was really weird because usually any movement in the room wakes me. I had nothing to say in my defense; I totally ruined our romantic evening. All the rest of the weekend, Adam was angry with me, saying things like, "We bothered my mother for nothing," and "I don't understand your priorities."

The new version will be installed in a couple hours, then this project will be over, and I'll have more time to sleep. I'll recover in a few days. It's just fatigue, I'm sure of it. I'm always like this before a version is released, especially when it's a big client like Danny. There are always endless phone calls, too, and emails around the clock. Absolute madness.

Everyone is still eating, so I allow myself to take off my shoes, the ones I bought in the last sale in Zara. They were surprisingly uncomfortable today, and my feet were numb by noon. What a stupid invention.

I go over my "to-do" list again and check that we haven't forgotten anything, noticing that despite taking off my shoes, my feet still feel numb. I can hardly feel the cold floor. I probably need some movement to get the blood flowing; I don't notice that I'm not moving enough when I'm so focused at work. I decide to go make some coffee to keep me awake through the version update.

Walking back into the room, coffee in hand, I see that my team is back. Anna smiles understandingly when she sees me walking barefoot across the room, and Ray and Dave pay no attention at all.

It's already getting dark, and most employees have gone home; only my team remains. We're waiting for final approvals to begin. Anna runs her regular playlist, and Dave wears his huge, noise-canceling, white headphones. It's as if I'm in a room filled with teenagers. The wired phone on my desk rings. The only one calling this line is Ilene.

"Hi, Ilene, is everything okay?"

"Hello, Karen," Ilene replies in her teacher's voice that already makes me feel like I did something wrong. "Olivia has a fever, and we can't find your Advil."

"I'm not sure we have any Advil. Did you take her temperature?" I ask since Ilene has a tendency to overreact. What terrible timing.

"Jacob's checking her now." I hear her murmur, "In what house with children is there no Advil?" Then she shouts, "Jacob, how high is her fever?"

I can't hear his answer as the pressure in my chest and my heartbeat both get stronger.

"One hundred and three. Poor child," Ilene says, and I realize this new version will be released without me.

My boss will kill me. Will already warned me once that parental responsibility is no excuse for dropping the ball at work, but what choice do I have? If I send Adam with her to the doctor, he won't be able to tell me anything later. I have to be the one to take her.

I look around at my team. How can I leave them in these critical moments? Where am I supposed to be now? What kind of mother would I be if I didn't go home to my baby girl? After all, Ilene didn't just call. She expects me to come back. If I stay at work, she won't forget it for years and will mention it at every family gathering. I can already see her at Olivia's wedding, telling how she raised my daughters and that even when they were sick, she took care of them. Even if Adam comes home, someone has to take her to the doctor, and someone has to stay with the girls. I don't see what other choice I have.

"I'm coming," I reply, and Ilene hangs up.

"I have to go. Call me if you need something," I tell Anna, who looks at me, stunned. I take my shoes in one hand, my bag in the other, and run toward the elevator.

This whole "dancing at two weddings" doesn't suit me today, and besides, I hate dancing.

11

RYLIE

"You have to hear this," I say to Noah when he finishes his shower. It's midnight, the boys are sleeping, and the house is quiet. I waited all day to talk to Noah in private. "I was at the grocery today, and Sammi said something surprising." I hope Noah will listen to me and not blow me off.

"What did that dumbbell tell you now?" Noah takes ironed boxers from his underwear drawer. This is what it looks like when my mom folds the laundry for us.

"Danielle asked you this week for money to buy candies for her school trip, right? Well, Sammi said she didn't buy it there. He even asked Don and he didn't see her either."

Noah is silent and continues to dry himself, but I know he hears me.

"Don't you think it's strange?" I ask again, hoping to get some kind of answer from him.

"No. So she bought it somewhere else. Who cares? She can buy what she wants where she wants." Noah returns to the shower and begins to shave.

I want to say that it does matter and that she can't do whatever she wants with our money, but I stay silent. There's no point in quarreling with him. She'll always win. Noah treats Danielle like she's a goddess; he almost worships her, unable to see who she really is or say one bad word about her. She's always right, and I'm always wrong.

Yesterday, Karen canceled a class again, and I went for a run instead, seizing the opportunity since my mom was here, helping out. When I returned, Danielle was locked in her room, the boys slept, and my mother was waiting for me in the kitchen.

"How was your run, honey?" Mommy asked, hugging me despite my sweat. "I made you a big tuna salad."

"Wow! Mommy, thank you!" I kissed her, noticing the kitchen was clean and tidy. The spices stood like soldiers, and the sink was empty and shiny. I sat down to eat the salad as Dad waited outside.

"Do you need anything else before I go?"

"No, Mom. Thank you! See you at dinner on Friday."

"Good night, honey." She kissed me on my head and opened the door. "The girl will come with you?"

"I think so."

"Don't worry, it will be okay. Good night." She smiled and closed the door quietly as she left.

I feel bad that my parents have to tolerate Danielle. Last time she was so intolerable, commenting on everything. Mommy noticed Danielle's blue hair, and I saw how she held back from saying anything. Sarah, Noah's ex-wife, was fine with it, so what could Noah say?

I'm tired of Danielle, and I've known her for only a few years. God knows how her parents have endured her for twelve years. Since she started middle school, she has so many problems. It all started after the holidays when she asked to transfer to another class, claiming she has trouble making friends.

Noah and Sarah went to her school and talked to the counselor. If I'd asked him to take time off work to go to Aiden's daycare, he would never do it. But for Danielle? He'll leave everything and run to her.

Since then he's also had nonstop conversations with Sarah about Danielle, which is driving me crazy. For years he complained that she was a horrible woman, critical and obsessive, and he couldn't stand it, but in recent months they write to each other all the time. Suddenly she's interested in his start-up and his investors, and she's also very interested in how the boys are. Really nice. If I say anything about it, Noah tells me that it's all in Danielle's best interest.

By the time Noah finishes shaving, I decide to check out Danielle's "candy" story. With the amount of money she gets from Noah, she buys a huge amount of candy, so where is it? If she eats too many sweets, she has a real problem, and it's so sad that her parents aren't willing to recognize it. I can see that she's become fuller, and I have to say something because Noah doesn't realize the long-term consequences of her body image.

I will not give up on it. I will have to act wisely, without quarreling with Noah. On the contrary, I'll keep him closer to me than ever. It might be silly, maybe childish, but every time I fight with him, I feel like she's winning.

I look at him as he brushes his teeth and smiles. He's still as handsome as ever, and his dimples melt my heart. He catches my gaze in the mirror and smiles his captivating smile. From that look I know I'm going to sleep an hour less tonight.

12

TARA

"What's going on with you? We haven't talked lately," I say to Karen when we meet at school. Her kids come out running and waving as if a year's passed since they saw her this morning.

"Nothing special. I'm really busy and I don't have a second to breathe." Karen bends and ties Olivia's laces.

"We must meet sometime. Maybe tonight? I got a new, expensive bottle of wine from a client as a thank-you for getting his loan approved. What do you say?"

"No way. I'm exhausted already and it's not five yet. Sometimes I fall asleep even before the bedtime story ... it's so embarrassing." Karen sighs, and I think it's been a long time since I've seen her smile.

"Still with that virus?" Karen's so fragile that sometimes I'm afraid she'll break if I hug her too strongly.

"No. I don't know. It's just getting worse. I don't know what I caught but I'm constantly tired and weak." Karen takes Olivia's hand and adds, "But we'll try to meet soon, I promise."

While I wait for Ella to come out, I watch Karen slowly walk to her minivan. I also work full-time and have four children, but occasionally I'm able to spend ten minutes to meet a friend.

Something is definitely wrong with her. She's always feeling bad and complaining. It might be emotional rather than physical.

Truthfully, it's not any fun talking to her lately. She might be depressed. Poor Adam. Who needs to see her sour face every day? He's such a charming guy.

Rylie also complains all the time that Karen's canceling on her at the last minute. Sometimes she doesn't even let her know and only calls the next day to apologize. It's strange and inappropriate for Karen to behave that way. Something's wrong with her. What could that be?

Years ago, I arranged for one of Juvi's friends to help her with the house. Every time I go to her house, the living room is full of laundry. I tried to suggest that she use the dryer and then fold everything immediately. Karen said it was unnecessary when you can just hang it to dry. Then she throws the dry clothes on the couch and doesn't fold them for days. It's as if Karen-at-work and Karen-at-home are two different people. At work she's punctual and organized. At home she loses her grip on things, kind of like a split personality.

I come home and find Ethan smoking on the balcony with Rick. I hate Rick. He's a nasty person. He's been taking Ethan to Bucharest from time to time. God knows what they do over there. I don't want to know.

I usually disapprove of the friends Ethan chooses for himself because he always sticks to all kinds of complicated people. Rick is a good example. There were suspicions that he was involved in smuggling artwork out of the country. Ethan said he hadn't been indicted in the end, but that didn't matter. Such types are always involved in something.

Ethan doesn't pay me any attention; he's completely immersed in Rick. I don't even know if he went to work today.

Mason hears that I'm home and yells at me from his room, "Mom, can I sleep at Jonathan's today?"

"Only if his mother allows it." There are mothers who don't allow sleepovers on school nights, but I don't care. It's not as if they study nuclear physics. Worst-case scenario, Mason will be a little tired tomorrow – maybe too tired to pick on Karen's daughter for once.

"She says it's okay. Can you take me now?"

"Sure, come on."

Although I haven't said hello to the girls yet, I'm glad to have the opportunity to avoid Ethan. As I take off my red high heels. I sigh in relief. I was stupid to wear them today. Walking over to the window, I notice the smell of cigars has already entered the house. Disgusting.

"Give it to her! Stop fighting already!" I hear Karen shouting at her girls and close the window, dimming the voices.

I look out at Ethan who doesn't even bother to care about his children. I wonder if he'll notice that Mason isn't sleeping at home tonight.

He's always known how to live life to the fullest. In retrospect, I should have realized he couldn't function normally, but his insistent courting broke me.

"I'll give you everything," he told me all the time. "Whatever you want."

And at every opportunity, he did. For each birth he bought me a different piece of jewelry: a diamond bracelet, matching necklace, and a pair of earrings. He always finds new, hot restaurants and surprises me every time with a trip for the weekend. He even sends my mother a huge bouquet of white flowers for her birthday every year. Well, maybe his secretary does that, but it's still his initiative.

On the other hand, he never believed in me. He laughed when I told him that I was offered the position of deputy branch manager at the bank. He said it was because there were no other candidates, so they got stuck with me. I faked a smile, as if laughing at his joke, but I knew he wasn't joking.

Lucky for me, I didn't listen to him. I accepted the job and informed him only when everything was settled and signed. If I hadn't done that, the role of the branch manager wouldn't be relevant. I needed a few years of experience as a deputy before I could offer my name for my dream job.

At the time, Ethan was an employee at a car dealership. The knowledge that his wife earned more than him and was more successful was unbearable to him. He always talks about "hitting the jackpot." In the meantime, he's just making trouble.

"Mom! Come on, Jonathan's waiting for me." Mason takes his bag and runs out of the house, not even trying to say goodbye to his father. Disappointed, I follow him and close the door.

In the Jeep, Mason starts playing a noisy game.

"How was school today?" I haven't returned his annoying teacher's call yet, even though she's called me several times. If it's important enough, she'll try again.

"Boring as usual," he says, over the sounds of explosions coming from his phone. "Shit," Mason says and I smile. He sounds like his father.

"The school year will be over soon," I say, encouraging mainly myself. Mason doesn't respond.

I drop him off at Jonathan's house and drive to the grocery store. Even Sammi's worn-out jokes are better than Rick's company.

"Don, look who came to visit us!" Sammi shouts, full of energy despite working from five in the morning. "Hello to the big manager, Mrs. Tara!"

"Hi Sammi," I say, and a smile manages to sneak away.

These two clowns always shout at each other. They seem to be busy, but they claim to know everything that goes on in the neighborhood. Once Sammi argued with some babysitter about the name of the boy she was watching, claiming his name was different. She eventually called the kid's mom, and it turned out Sammi was right. The boy had a second name. The conversation delayed all the other shoppers at the grocery store, but Sammi was pleased with himself and told everyone in the store about it two weeks later.

"How's beautiful Juvi? We haven't seen her in a long time." Sammi vigorously cleans the cash register while I struggle to pull out a shopping cart.

"Very well, helping me with Emma. She has less time for shopping. It looks like next time we'll order a delivery."

"Whatever you want."

Ronnie goes to help Don, and I continue to wander the narrow aisles. I don't really know what I need except to get away from home. I put milk in the cart. One always needs more milk. I walk slowly and add pasta and tomato paste. Juvi will prepare pasta for the children tomorrow. If I had the strength, I'd prepare it myself.

The kids just want pasta, pizza, and hot dogs, and Juvi can do that. I pass by the beers and decide not to buy any. Maybe if we don't have beer in the house, Ethan will move his ass and actually do something.

I park the Jeep but stay in the car, going through Facebook a bit. Karen's gate opens, and I want to go out and say hello, but it's not her.

A tall man comes out of her house. It's not Adam.

13

KAREN

On Saturday morning we decide to have breakfast in the neighborhood café located in a small shopping center between the grocery and the place where Tara has her nails done. On Saturdays, the place is crowded with exhausted parents who want to spend a few hours by themselves, and with families trying to enjoy a nice breakfast.

"Mia doesn't want to come to your parents' today," I tell Adam as he pours me some water. At least this time he didn't insist on ordering mineral water.

"Why? She didn't come last time either. My mother's going to be offended."

"Your mother would be offended at some point anyway. Mia's friend, June, invited her for a sleepover, and it's a really good sign. It's important to strengthen the social part of her life." It's still unclear to me why such a beautiful, talented girl finds herself constantly alone.

"Okay ,whatever. I'll talk to my mom later. Don't tell her anything when we get back home," he says eventually.

Obviously, the conversation with Ilene will be unpleasant. She'll take Mia's absence personally, as if she did something wrong and this is some kind of punishment. Her reactions are classic, as if she took an advanced drama course at the University of Mothers-in-law.

Anything can offend Ilene. If I don't take another piece of the cake she baked, she'll be offended because it means it's not good enough. If the girls don't wear what she bought, she's offended and says she won't buy them anything ever again. Because she helps us so much, I have patience with her. After all, these are the only grandparents we have for the girls.

"What do you say about a night in a villa for my birthday? We'll invite some friends and maybe arrange some activities. Nothing terribly pompous." I look at Adam, who is busy spreading French cheese on a piece of bread.

"Whatever you want, I'm a flexible guy," he replies with a smile.

"I'll try to find something that won't be too expensive," I think out loud. "If we preorder, we might find good deals, but maybe not on a weekend. It will probably cost less."

We return home, Ilene leaves, and Adam goes out with the girls to do the weekly shopping, one of the few chores I save for him exclusively. I only do the urgent shopping at Sammi's grocery store where Don carries my bags to my car.

The girls' shoes are scattered everywhere, the sink is full of dishes, and the clothes the maid washed a few days ago are waiting for someone to fold them. I have no energy to do anything. I feel like I've returned from a marathon, not a breakfast.

I have an hour before Adam returns with the girls from the supermarket, and I decide to consult Dr. Google about this fatigue. Too many strange things have been going through my body during the last year. Deep down I feel that something's wrong, even though all my tests came back normal. It's as if I got a bug and I can't find its source or fix it.

If I tell Adam that I'm looking for an answer on Google, he'll tell me I'm always pessimistic and thinking the worst. So yes, I'll admit (solely to myself) that I'm a little bit traumatized by what happened to my parents. With them, the worst-case scenario became reality, so he can't blame me for wanting to rule out the cancer threat.

A few years after my mom passed from breast cancer, Dad started to feel strange things in his hands and feet. At one point he couldn't raise his right hand well, and we later discovered he had a brain tumor. We were shocked that a perfectly healthy man who had never been sick beyond the common cold had terminal cancer. I must make sure everything is really okay with me.

I sit down with my laptop and type "leg numb" into Google. A lot of links pop up, and I click on one called "Why is my leg numb? 6 possible causes of leg numbness." Maybe I'll find the information about the tests I need to have. I smile. The first cause is sitting too much. Ilene will definitely agree with that.

I write "fatigue" in the search bar and get a list of lifestyle factors that causes it. I read the recommendation to check for a lack of iron and for thyroid problems, but I already had all that tested. I started taking iron supplements that didn't change anything and just added more symptoms – abdominal pain and constipation.

The smell of fried onions starts to fill the house: Tara's cooking, and the smell coming from her house makes my stomach come alive. I think she also bakes a cake, which smells great. I could ask for the recipe, but it won't be helpful. Baking it will only frustrate me – and Adam – even more.

Next, I search for "weakness in hands," another symptom I've been feeling lately, and I get lots of results. One is a brain tumor, and I feel nauseous as I read the headline. Thinking about it, when Dad got sick, I also felt tired. There were days when I didn't feel well at all, and I occasionally got up with leg pain that lasted for several hours and disappeared as it came. It was certainly due to the pressure I was experiencing at the time. Two young girls, a full-time job, and a sick father. It was far beyond reasonable.

I go through the search results, and one of them is very surprising: MS symptoms. The name's familiar, but I know nothing about this disease. Curious, I click on the link and start reading aloud.

"MS symptoms are variable and unpredictable. Multiple sclerosis causes brain and spinal cord lesions. Symptoms vary from person to person and the same person at different times." There is a long list of symptoms that ends up with a full disability. This is a serious illness. It's probably not what I have because if it was something that serious, someone would have found it by now.

I go back to the main screen and read some more about neuropathy that causes the numbness of the legs and the weakness. One cause is a lack of vitamin B. It makes much more sense already. I send Adam a message to buy me a multivitamin at the pharmacy. It will probably improve my feelings in a few weeks. After all, with my diet, it's a miracle I survive at all. Even my team says I eat like a schoolgirl – rice and chicken. It's humiliating to tell them that this is what Ilene prepares for the girls, so I eat it too.

If I had to feed myself, it would probably end up being a sandwich with Nutella.

14

RYLIE

"Do you think I can ask her about it?" I whisper to Tara at the end of her workout while we walk out to the street. Tara rarely arrives for training during the afternoon.

"Obviously, sweetie. After all, she lives with you. You should be able to talk to her," she says, smiling that big smile of hers. Everything seems so simple with her.

I frown. "I don't feel as if I can talk to her like that." Now that I think about it, I've never had a normal conversation with Danielle. I walk with Tara to her house, and we stand on the sidewalk.

"Listen," Tara says, "I have no adolescents at home, thank goodness, but I think you should just go to her when both of you are able to talk patiently and calmly."

I'm about to thank her when Karen comes out of her house, followed by a really tall guy with dense little curls. She accompanies him to a car parked in front of her house, and they hug for a few seconds before he gets in the car and drives off. When she sees us, she waves and smiles, and then, without waiting for a response, she goes back home. It's so strange that she didn't come to chat.

All the nonsense with Danielle goes out of my mind, and I ask Tara, "Who was that guy? Do you know him?"

"No. But I think I've seen him here before," she whispers in my ear, as if revealing a secret.

"Why are we whispering?" I whisper back to her. This is the most interesting thing that's happened to me since we moved here.

"I don't like talking behind Karen's back, so I'll just say this isn't the first time I've seen him at her house when Adam wasn't there," Tara says, her gaze not leaving Karen's house.

"This whole story doesn't make sense to me. I know Karen, and she doesn't look like someone who would betray her husband – especially not Adam. He adores her."

"Maybe I'm just exaggerating," Tara says. "Anyway, Karen's our friend and we're always on her side. I have to go inside now. Tell me what Danielle says about the sweets."

"Sure. Thanks again."

It's hard for me to believe Tara's suspicions. Karen and Adam are the perfect couple. He's been so supportive of her with all her problems lately, and she constantly tells me how much he helps her with the girls and how he does everything around the house. Truly a rare man.

I enter the house with a lot of noise inside my mind: the gossip about Karen, the sweets, the talk with Danielle. I peel the vegetables for dinner and get an annoying text from Noah: "I'll be late today, babe. Tomorrow I fly to London for three days. I must finish the draft of the contract tonight! We got an amazing offer!!!"

I hate his start-up more than ever.

Mom sits with Thomas and Aiden in the living room and watches another episode of *PAW Patrol*. Aiden's absolutely confident by now that all dogs talk and drive cars. Even Mom knows all the characters.

"Mommy, Noah's flying tomorrow. Can you stay here tonight and help me for three days?" I ask.

"Sure, sweetie, whatever you want. I'll tell Dad."

"Thanks, Mommy ."

I'm so lucky to have her. Maybe if Noah manages to sell his company, I'll have someone like Juvi to help me around the house, then I can go out whenever I want. We might also buy a bigger house instead of renting this one.

Maybe.

Heavy footsteps come up the path. Here we go again. Danielle storms home with energies that could make a lion seek shelter. She goes upstairs without saying hello, as if I'm not standing here. If Noah was here, she would have said something to show him how much she tries so she could blame me for everything that happens. She's a monster.

Mommy looks at me and shrugs her shoulders. She also seems to be getting discouraged. I take a deep breath and try to think about how I can do what Tara suggested earlier. Maybe now, since Mom can look after the boys, it's a good time to talk to Danielle. How am I supposed to have a conversation with this girl who doesn't even see me? Everything Tara said might be suitable for someone else – a normal adolescent, not Danielle.

It's been bothering me for too long. I keep trying to figure out what she's doing with all this money she takes from Noah. Where does she hide all her sweets? I searched her room and found nothing but an empty package under her bed. This is probably what's left of everything she's already eaten. The search itself was a horrible experience as her room was dirty and messy. I'm just waiting for her to go back to her mom's so I can vacuum and clean in there. How can she live like that?

Thomas curls up with Mommy on the couch, and Aiden's painting Rider's red hat. Each time he paints a different drawing in the booklet Noah bought him when he was in New York. The living room table – and pieces of apple he's been eating – are covered with red paint from Aiden's fingers.

Noah will arrive late tonight, and it might be an opportunity to talk to Danielle without him being here to protect her. My stomach churns from stress. I just want this conversation to be over. It's now or never; if I don't do it now, I won't have the courage later.

Danielle is closed up in her room, so I knock on the door with my fake confidence and wait for her permission to enter. I want to start the conversation without quarreling about entering her room without her majesty's approval.

"What?" she growls, and I carefully open the door.

"May I come in?" I ask, trying to start the conversation calmly.

"If you must," she replies, not even looking at me.

I enter the lioness's cage and close the door, approaching her cautiously, as if trying not to frighten her. I look for a place to sit, but her chair is full of clothes. I lift them gently and put them on the table with her pens, notebooks, multiple bottles of nail polish in all colors, and a red lipstick. Why does a twelve-year-old need a lipstick?

Danielle acts like I'm not there. Like I don't exist. I take another deep breath and sit down. Maybe that will make me seem less intimidating. She lies on the bed, her red curls spreading out on her pillow as she stares at her iPhone screen. Every few seconds the song in the background changes.

"I want to ask you something." I stick to the exact speech I practiced in my head.

Danielle is silent. I remain invisible to her.

"I want to know if there's anything I can help with. I mean, maybe you need help with something." I hold my phone in my hand like a lifeline.

"Sure," she replies, "you can just leave. That would be very helpful," she says with an artificial, wicked smile.

The truth is that this is exactly what I want to do, but I know that if Danielle isn't treated as soon as possible, she could cause irreversible damage to her body. I know it. I learned about eating disorders as part of my nutrition studies, and I know how to identify it. The denial is part of this disease.

"Listen, I know you're going through a difficult period, but eating candy isn't healthy for your body – especially during adolescence. Processed sugar actually causes long—"

"Uhhh! Just shut up and go away!" she screams, her reaction shocks me. This behavior is the reason her parents are afraid to deal with her. Her face goes red, and her freckles almost disappear.

"Eating junk will hurt only you and nobody else. If you want to talk to someone—"

"I don't want to talk to you! So shut up and get out of my room!" she barks at me.

I decide to try a different approach. "I was your age once. I know how difficult it is—"

"You don't understand anything! Just get out of here!" She stands up nervously and opens the door, this time looking in my direction. I feel the hatred coming out of her eyes like poisoned arrows.

"I won't go out until you admit that you have a problem. Your dad knows that too. I'm not willing to buy so many sweets for you anymore!" I stand in front of her to make her understand I won't give up on her.

"Leave me alone, bitch!" Danielle screams, and I'm in a complete shock. I can't say anything. I don't know what to do.

She grabs her bag from the floor and runs down the stairs. I'm barely out of the room when I hear the front door slam.

I go downstairs, and Mommy looks at me as Aiden and Thomas continue to watch Chase rescue someone.

"You have to get along with her. A girl shouldn't talk like that. Lucky your father didn't hear her."

"I don't have to do anything. I tried and now Noah and her poor mother will take care of it the way they want to." I sit down next to Aiden, my body trembling with anger. I lost control completely. My phone rings, and I see Noah's name on the screen. Behind his name is a picture from our trip to New Zealand.

"Hi, babe," I answer, hoping he's calling to tell me that the trip was shortened or maybe even canceled.

"Why did Danielle tell me you banished her from our home? What's going on? It's impossible to have one evening without some sort of drama between you," he says impatiently, and with every word I lose my confidence. "I'm stressed enough about the trip as it is. I don't need this nonsense now."

"I didn't banish her," I say, signaling Mom to stay with the boys. I go upstairs so none of them will hear me.

"So why did she call and say she's on the street?" It's amazing that he always believes everything she says.

"She's just making a scene for attention. I only tried to talk to her about the sweets." I close the bedroom door behind me.

"Why? What good was that supposed to do? I don't understand you sometimes. Leave it. I'll talk to her about it. It's not urgent. I'm asking you to go outside and bring her home. It doesn't make sense for her to be out there alone."

So maybe she should stop running away like that, I want to tell him but remain silent. One-zero, advantage to Danielle.

"Okay, babe," I say after a few seconds of quiet as Noah breathes nervously.

I'm not at all sure she'll agree to come back inside, but for Noah's sake, I'm ready to try. I really hate to fight with him before he flies.

"Thanks, babe," he says, calmer now. "I know she's not easy. I'll come home as soon as I can."

"All right, I'll send my mom to bring her in. Maybe she'll listen to her." I know that if I ask Danielle, it will end poorly.

"Great idea. I'll call you on the way home. We're still working on the presentation for tomorrow."

"Do you think this is a real offer this time?" Because of all the mess with Danielle, I forgot that this trip was really important to Noah and that there was a chance that this time he really would sell his company. The big exit is within reach.

"There's a lot of potential here." I hear the enthusiasm in his voice again.

"I'm so happy! Good luck, babe!"

"Love you, babe," Noah says, making me smile, but the smile disappears with the realization that now I have to deal with Danielle.

I return to Mommy, who hugs me and asks anxiously, "What will we do with the girl?"

"There's nothing to do. She's mad at me. She told Noah she was outside. Can you ask her to come in?"

"Whatever you want, honey," Mommy says, smiling at me.

I look at them through the kitchen window and see that they're talking, though I can't hear what they're saying to each other.

"Mom, they did it!" Aiden yells from the living room as Thomas applauds the brave puppies.

"Well done, sweetie," I say without taking my eyes off Mom and Danielle.

Danielle stands and walks toward the house without looking at my mom at all. Mom follows her, and when she sees me through the window, she smiles at me with a triumphant look. Danielle enters and goes to her room without saying a word or looking in my direction. As usual.

"What did you tell her?" I ask quietly after the door to the Danielle's room closes behind her.

"Nothing special. I just told her that if she came in, then the next time I come, I'll make her the pancakes she loves."

I want to tell her that with all the sweets Danielle eats every night, I'm not sure that pancakes are a good idea.

15

KAREN

Adam has already taken the girls this morning, so I can take my time getting ready for work. I'm standing in front of the shoe drawer, trying to find a pair of shoes that I'll be comfortable wearing. My favorite high heels are just too painful.

I told Tara that my feet suddenly went numb in the middle of a presentation to a new client, and she said it was probably because of the heels. She recommended that I buy better quality shoes where she buys hers. When I went to the website she sent me and saw the prices, I almost had a heart attack. Buying there won't help my health, that's for sure.

I leave the house slowly, heading for my car, mentally prepared for a long hour of traffic jams awaiting the lazy who leave home too late. A cruel modern punishment.

Lately, Adam has been angry with me because I'm always tired, and he's expressing his anger by being indifferent toward me. He claims I'm overloading things and that's why I'm exhausted.

Not long ago, he asked me if I wanted to join him for a bike ride on a Saturday morning. He said the girls could sleep at his parents on Friday so that we could wake up early and head for the forest. I told him that I'd like to do that, but I couldn't.

"But you've had everything tested and you have no problem. Let's do something to boost your energy."

"Give me energy by letting me sleep, not cycling."

"You can't sit at home all the time," he said.

I got upset and sent him to sleep at his parents with the girls. At least he didn't wake me up at five the next morning.

The elevator opens, and with great effort, I pull open the heavy glass door. It's only when I see Anna's startled face and everyone in the conference room that I remember. How could I forget we have a toast this morning to celebrate the end of our project – the system we developed for the biggest insurance company in the country? How stupid can I be?

I place my bag on the secretary's desk and enter the conference room quietly, Anna walking a few steps behind me. Everyone's talking and laughing, and I hope no one notices my late arrival. But my attempt fails.

"Hello, Karen, where were you? Everyone's been asking about you." Will comes up to me with a plastic glass full of a bubbling beverage. I can feel that I'm blushing, and my heart is pounding like crazy.

"Sorry, something personal came up," I reply, hoping he'll think it's some female issues and lose interest.

"We thought you'd want to be here and say a few words," he continues. "After all, it's your team's client and your team's work."

"Never mind," I say. "Next time."

Someone comes to congratulate Will, and I seize the opportunity to get away. I go around and talk to as many people as possible so that everyone will notice that I came.

After my hello round, I slip out of the conference room into my aquarium. I must have a few minutes of silence to settle my thoughts before the whole team returns. Lately, this has been happening to me a lot, this forgetfulness, as if I've had a glass or two of red wine.

What I won't forget is the time I forgot to pick up Mia from her math tutor. I found her standing on the sidewalk outside his house, looking very angry.

"Mom, where have you been?" she screamed as soon as she entered the back seat and slammed the door. "I've been waiting for you for hours!"

"It's been ten minutes and I'm really sorry," I said. "I've been delayed."

If I'd told her that I forgot her, she would have continued screaming, and then she would have told everyone, especially Ilene. I fixed everything with a short stop at Sammi's grocery store. A bar of chocolate and vanilla ice cream did the trick – a relatively small price to pay compared to years of emotional therapy at an overpriced rate per hour.

Forgetting things at work is a much bigger problem that ice cream can't fix. On Sunday night two weeks ago, I almost had a heart attack. I went through my emails to look for a confirmation for Olivia's summer camp and found an email I missed. My heart was pounding madly, and my hands were shaking from stress.

The client had asked when he could see his fixed website. I realized that not only had I not passed on his comments to my team to handle, I also completely forgot that he had sent a list of comments. It was as if his email evaporated from my head.

It was the first time something like that ever happened to me. If that had happened to one of my staff, I would have sent them home in five minutes and sent their stuff later in a box.

"How can I tell him I forgot?" I asked Adam hysterically. "William will kill me – worse, he'll fire me!" Images of me sitting at job interviews ran through my mind. How would I explain why I was looking for a new position? Between interviews, I would be home all day, having to prepare a hot, nutritious meal every day for lunch. All I would do is help the girls with their homework, and I'd have to admit I don't remember long division.

Horror gripped me as I thought what Ilene would say. "She can't do her job either, so what exactly is your wife good at?" If she tried to teach me how to prepare her casserole, I thought, I'd have no choice but to run away from home.

"Can you do it yourself?" Adam asked as he watched me walk back and forth to the kitchen, mumbling to myself.

"Sure. It's not complicated." I stopped walking.

"How long will it take you?" Adam was the only one who could get me out of the spin I was getting into.

"I have no idea." I returned to the computer and searched hysterically for the poor customer's previous email. It turned out he had been waiting for his updated website for two weeks. "I'm so stupid! How could I forget about this email?"

"Maybe you can do it from home tonight?" Adam can work all night on a case if needed, but I'm usually in bed by nine. Every time we watch an episode together in the evening, I fall asleep within minutes, and he has to give me an update the next day ("He left, she cried, and that's how it ended").

"No way. I'm so tired." I was completely discouraged and mostly disappointed in myself. It's totally not typical of me to forget something like that.

"Tomorrow morning then. And answer his email only after you finish everything. He doesn't need to know you've seen the mail today, right?" These were moments when I was happy I married a lawyer. I hugged and kissed him before running back to the computer to print the damn email that had eluded me.

"Great! Tomorrow morning you'll take the girls out and I can work." I had to finish as early as possible before someone else realized I screwed up.

But although I was tired, I didn't fall asleep that night. I lay in bed, trying to think about why this was happening to me all the time. Now, I think it's getting worse. Today I forgot the toast. Last month I forgot the pasta for two hours on the stove (it turned into a block of pasta), and I burned the pizza in the oven (how hard is it to heat a frozen pizza?). I forgot to pick up Mia. I forget everything.

Adam always laughs at me about it, but I can't joke about it anymore. It's happened so many times in such a short time. Where did the organized girl with the to-do list disappear to? The girl that planned everything down to the last sub-subsection. In a few months I'll be forty, and I feel like I have the body and mind of a sixty-year-old woman.

Through the transparent glass walls, I see everyone else eating bagels in the conference room. Opening my browser again, I type into Google's search field, "Numbness in the legs, feeling of burning feet, fatigue." What else? I'm probably forgetting even how I feel. So many things bother me. I add "memory impairment."

I get the same results as last time. Those associated with "brain tumor" remind me of Dad and make me shiver. The other options aren't very encouraging either: Alzheimer's, multiple sclerosis, and other terrible diseases. I close the browser in despair.

Something's wrong. I must go see a neurologist. I know that for sure now. I may even have to have some tests done to see what's going on inside my "blonde brain," as Adam refers to my memory issues.

I cry, and these modern glass walls don't quite fit my current mood. I quickly wipe my eyes, realizing that I must rule out these horrors. In the HMO app, I make an appointment for the first available neurologist in the area.

I remember something Ilene told me when Mia told her I burnt her birthday cake: "It's either psychological or neurological, but something is wrong with your head."

Ilene's right. And if I think she's right about something, then something's really wrong with my head.

16

TARA

On the way to the bank, my head is full of thoughts about Ethan and our relationship. Two years ago, it was almost as bad as it is now. We were constantly fighting, and everything he did annoyed me. I couldn't tolerate his friends anymore, and he started going out to all kinds of places without me and stopped sending me romantic messages like he used to. We'd gone days without exchanging a word, and I was already imagining how I'd announce that it was over, that there was no reason to continue with this relationship.

But then he surprised me and took me to Tuscany for my birthday, and I returned pregnant with Emma. The hormones, the excitement, and especially the surprise of a fourth pregnancy pushed away any thoughts of divorce. We returned to a more pleasant routine, maybe not like it used to be during our early years, but it was bearable.

Time passed, though, and the hormones returned to normal. Emma is now one year old, and I feel sane again, back to my old self. Unfortunately, Ethan's also back to his old self.

I'm having those feelings of disappointment again, disappointment that he doesn't change, doesn't mature, doesn't listen.

My heart is filled with all of it. I know I'm not supposed to compromise. After all, when the children grow up, only the two of us will remain in our empty nest. Even Juvi will leave one day and go back to her family in the Philippines, and then what? What common ground will we have left? How much can you talk about restaurants? We have nothing else to talk about.

I shouldn't do anything irreversible without a serious discussion. We have four kids, and I can't hurt them and change their whole life because their dad acts like a child. I knew who he was when we got married; it didn't come as a surprise to me. I knew he liked spending time with his shady friends, people with whom I wouldn't choose to hang out – like this Alex, who I hate.

"Don't you have your own home?" I would hint at him, as if joking. Every time he comes to visit Ethan he stays until after midnight – just like that, in the middle of the week, as if no one has to get up for work the next morning.

He also screams when he laughs and wakes Emma up, but he just smiles his creepy smile and answers the same again and again, "There's no place like your house, Tara." I could just kill him.

Ethan admires him. He sits with Alex, fascinated, laughing at every sexist joke, getting excited about Alex's stupid ideas, believing everything Alex says. Ethan ignores the disruption to our family and the fact that I have to get up early, organize the kids, and go to work. Not everyone can show up at work when they want to. I told Ethan that there was something fishy about Alex – nothing specific, just something. I don't know why, but I don't like it when he's around the kids.

I'm late for work and have to put everything aside and concentrate. I'm entering the temporary branch we moved to where workers still wander everywhere, speaking all sorts of languages, none of which I can understand. I place my bag on my dirty desk and move the computer mouse. Nothing happens. Perhaps in all the chaos no one noticed that I was late.

"Nothing works here!" I shout.

No one's excited about it. The service desk opens in the afternoon, and all systems need to be up and running. Erika, the smiling secretary to the branch manager, approaches me. She's as calm as if she were anywhere else but here, indifferent to the banging and shouting.

"The poor technicians worked all night, and they'll connect the computers soon. The phones work, but the queue monitor doesn't." Erika tries to calm me down, which is nice but ineffective. Nothing can help now. I'm too tired and too upset. Erika pulls another empty box from the table and puts it on the floor. A cloud of dust rises around it.

"But there's no Internet. No emails. Nothing!" I say in despair.

My clock from the previous office leans against the wall, waiting for one of the thousands of workers to kindly hang it up. It's almost noon. This day is completely wasted.

"Do you want me to bring you something to drink? I'm going to make some coffee," Erika continues to try, knowing that there's no point in talking to me before I drink my coffee.

"Thanks. I'm coming with you. There's nothing to do here anyway."

On the way to the kitchen, I scan my surroundings. Everyone's running around, trying to finish their work as quickly as possible. Tools are scattered on the filthy floor. The smell of ammonia is so strong that my headache is getting worse.

"What have you decided? Will you apply for it? It seems to me that managing the branch would be right for you," Erika asks in the temporary kitchenette we organized.

"I don't know. I'm a little stressed about dealing with branch management. I've only been a deputy for about four years." I make my second cup of coffee for today – if you can call it coffee. The machine is still in the crate, and I'm forced to use bags of instant coffee. Disgusting.

I've been contemplating this job for the last two months, having heard about it from Erika before it was even published. I have a couple of months to think about it. I've lost some good sleep on that as well.

"If anyone can do it, it's you. You'll be great, and rumor has it that your chances are excellent." Erika pours low-fat milk into her coffee and stirs it slowly.

Erika has all the right connections in the right places. Shorter than me, she's small and energetic. Her short curls, always in shades of red, give her a playful look. Maybe we get along well because we both love to do our job with as few distractions as possible.

I didn't tell Ethan about the job opportunity because I knew exactly what he'd say: "Why do you need it? What's wrong with what you do now?" He doesn't like change.

"I'll think about it," I tell Erika. "I'm going out to make some calls. Let me know when it's possible to work."

I decide to take the time to go through my emails on my mobile – a chance to have some connection with the outside world. After all, the bank's work can't stop because of this transition ... or because of Ethan.

I got an email from the board of the bank about the new security system and try to figure out what they want, reading it again and again from the top, but I've lost all my ability to concentrate today. Since all the computers are down, it's not relevant yet. No one can hack them now. Maybe I should ask Karen about it. She'd definitely understand it.

I open Facebook just to clear my head. Fall events are coming. Karen organized an event for the community – flower activities at the community center. She never gets tired of organizing activities, as if the sole purpose of her life is to engage people during their free time. Last fall, we planted trees and decorated plants. It was Saturday noon! Who sets something on Saturday at noon?

Nowadays, as she plans her birthday, she's unstoppable, organizing a crazy party for herself at a luxurious villa for all her friends. I already confirmed we'd be at the party, and it looks like we'll be about ten people. She asked everyone to reserve the date, although it's not for a few more months.

Lately I've hardly met up with her. She kind of disappeared on me. Maybe it has to do with the guy I saw at her house. She didn't say anything about him, but since she disappeared, he comes more often (I see him every few days, especially when Adam's away).

The last time I talked to Karen was a month ago at a picnic in the park. Mia didn't exchange a word with Mason all morning, as if they hadn't been together since kindergarten; she preferred being with the little girls. Besides that, the other kids got along great.

Even the men behaved surprisingly well. Initially, they talked about work, but later they discovered a common hobby – cycling – and started to compare equipment, accessories, and performance, not that I ever saw Ethan riding his bike. He bought it mainly because it was the hot thing a year ago. Everyone began to ride, so he had to have it too. Now he has the most elaborate model he could find, but only the dust rides it nowadays.

I try to stop my thoughts about Ethan and return to Facebook. Someone's looking for a private fitness trainer in the neighborhood, so I highly recommend Rylie. Maybe it will compensate her for the lesson I canceled on her last week. I planned on going, but the minute I got home, four kids were on me with their nonstop demands: a cake for Emily because she was the star of the week; a presentation on the Eiffel Tower for

Mason; and most importantly, building a model of Noah's Ark with Ella. I still have glue on my Gucci watch band. Emma was teething and just needed my attention.

Ethan, of course, refused to stop watching the soccer game ("This is the English league, I tell you."), so I gave up on him. I had no chance.

In the WhatsApp group of Mason's basketball team, someone's looking for a parent who can carpool for tonight's practice. I don't understand what Mason likes about this stupid sport. Ethan really pushed him to join after Mason strongly refused to join the football club. God forbid Ethan's only son didn't do some kind of sport – and preferably a competitive one. Luckily he's only ten and still not in the league, which meets three times a week. There's no way Ethan would help.

In the branch there's still a total mess, so I open the financial news app. The quarterly reports of the banks are about to be published any day now.

Thankfully, I'm sitting on the paint box the workers left at the entrance. Otherwise, I would have passed out on the floor after reading the title of the article appearing on my screen.

17

KAREN

"Something's wrong," I explain to the neurologist, who seems unimpressed with the list of symptoms I prepared in advance so that I could give him a printed copy. "I'm weak and tired, I'm dizzy sometimes, and my right hand is weak. My feet get numb if I walk too fast, and I just feel like I'm not myself lately."

"You're probably just stressed. Maybe you should try taking something soothing. I'm sure that within a few weeks you'll feel better," the neurologist says confidently without even examining me.

"I Googled my symptoms and they fit multiple sclerosis or a brain tumor. Maybe that's what I have?" I just can't go on like this. I'm going crazy.

"No need, you don't have MS. I have patients with MS, and I'm sure you don't have it. And it's not a brain tumor either. Nothing's wrong with you. It's just anxiety. Strengthen your muscles and take the pills I'm going to prescribe for you."

"What anxiety? How does it relate to anxiety?" I ask, feeling somewhat relieved. Anxiety is fixable. This cloud hovering over me for the past few months is starting to fade.

Every time I felt something strange, I Googled it to see if it was listed as a neurological problem. I was already thinking about the Filipino who would take care of me when I was in a wheelchair, and Adam laughed at me for finding an excuse to avoid cooking for our grandchildren.

"I see in your medical record that your mother was diagnosed with cancer around your age, so you're probably just getting anxious. It makes you have those weird symptoms."

"But I don't feel anxious," I try to convince him. "I just feel weak. I have blurred vision sometimes and my feet get numb. How is that related to anxiety?" In a way I want him to convince me.

"You suppress your anxiety, but your body feels it," he says emphatically, handing me the signed pages. "Start with the pills and let's see in a few weeks if all these things have gone away."

I don't agree with his anxiety theory, but I leave with a great sense of relief. On the way to work, I call Adam to tell him what the neurologist just told me.

"Nonsense," Adam says, "I know you and it's not anxiety. But take the pills and we'll see."

Adam really knows me, and I trust him completely, but I'm still not sure he gets the heart of my problem. Sometimes it's convenient for him to believe in Ilene's diagnosis. After all, it's common knowledge that a science teacher is just like a doctor, only without the certification. Ilene diagnosed me as overindulgent and lazy with a slight allergy to order and cleanliness. I'm sure she'd also agree that the solution is reeducation, preferably at her house. She fears that it's contagious and that the girls, God forbid, might catch it too.

"So what should I do about it? I feel I'm becoming less focused and I'm constantly tired. It's really hard for me to live like that. With all my screw-ups at work, I'm going to get myself fired."

"Go to another doctor. Maybe he'll find what's wrong with you. Maybe Tara knows someone good."

"Great idea. You see? I couldn't even think of it myself. My mind's a complete disaster."

"You're lucky to have me." I can hear that he's smiling.

"Totally. Tell me something. What horrible disease must I have to persuade your mother to stop trying to teach me how to cook?"

"Very funny. What do you want to do about the villa? I can book it for the date of your birthday on Friday."

"I'm not sure. What did they tell you about the price?"

"If we book Friday, we must pay for two nights, but I have an idea. On Thursday there's a possibility for one night and it's much cheaper. What do you say?"

"I say book it!" Adam always knows exactly what I need to hear.

18

TARA

The real estate entrepreneur Alex Dvornikov is suspected of fraud. Mr. Dvornikov will be brought for his hearing in front of a judge later today. It's suspected that Mr. Dvornikov has been marketing apartments in fake real estate projects in various parts of the country, without having the lands in his possession, while presenting false information to potential buyers.

My head feels heavy as I read, and dizziness accompanied by nausea almost makes me fall from the paint box. I keep reading the article, and it's hard because my hands are shaking. For a moment I have hopes that it's another Alex, but his picture – he's sitting smugly in his blue Uniqlo coat – leaves no doubt. This is the same fucking Alex who came to us and would not leave. I call Ethan, my hands still shaking.

Before he utters even one word, I'm already shouting, "Have you seen the article? They arrested your idiot friend."

"What are you talking about?" He sounds sleepy.

"I'm talking about Alex! The police arrested him!" I can't

breathe. I can see Karen is calling. She can wait. The whole world can wait.

"No way. I don't believe it," Ethan says, a little more awake. "Wait, I'm looking for it."

Could he still be home? Luckily, I asked Juvi to take the kids to school this morning. If it was up to him, they'd probably still be in the living room in front of the TV.

"Shit! Shit!" Ethan says.

"You're such a screw-up! You gave him all that money for nothing! For something that doesn't exist!"

Erika peeps through the filthy glass as I walk back and forth at the entrance to the bank, trying unsuccessfully to relax.

"I'll talk to him. He'll give us the money back. He's my friend." I hear in his voice that he's still in bed, which just annoys me further.

"Are you stupid or do you just act like one? What is this nonsense, 'He's my friend'? Are you in kindergarten? How can you talk to him? He's in custody, I tell you!" The reality doesn't confuse him.

"Okay. They'll let him out on bail."

"Do you understand the mistake you've made? I told you not to give him money before you got all the documents from the lawyer. Do you know to whom you transferred the money?" I told him a thousand times, and he wouldn't listen. He always knows better than everyone else. Always. He's lucky not to be near me right now. I could hit him with a hammer, and there are quite a few around me.

"The trustee is someone Alex gave me. If you don't take risks, you don't get anywhere," he says, repeating his silly, irresponsible mantra again.

"Do you listen to the stupid things you say?" I emphasize every word. I'm about to have a heart attack, right here between the paint box and the dusty handrail. "Just don't tell me you're part of it. Don't dare to say that you knew about the fraud." If he admits it, the police won't need to arrest him. I'll deliver him to them myself.

"Of course not. And I didn't sign anything. Don't worry," he says, and I hear his usual confidence. He's back.

"What do you mean you didn't sign anything? You signed the contract with Alex, right? You told me you signed it."

"I told you I was supposed to go to a lawyer to sign, but I also told you he postponed the meeting. I'm telling you again ... you have nothing to worry about."

"If you didn't sign the contract, then why did you transfer the money? You're so stupid! Stupid and a liar!" I scream. "How can you tell me not to worry? We lost all our money! Do you understand what happened? We won't see our money again! You lied to me. You gave money without a signed contract. I just can't believe you did it!" I shout, but Ethan doesn't answer anymore as Erika looks at me through the window again.

In a trembling voice, as clearly as I can, I say, "You're just a liar and I can't live like this anymore. Do you understand me?" I hang up the call before he has time to answer. There's nothing he can say that will calm me down.

I walk from side to side, sweating and shaking. It took us many years to save that money. Now we have to start all over again from scratch, years of hard work dumped into the trash – years when I worked late, when I barely managed to give the kids a good-night kiss. Years of events I missed because I was at the bank. Years that I worked until the moment I entered the delivery room and didn't extend my leave so that I wouldn't harm my promotion. Years of effort to prove myself to my superiors – those who thought that because I was a mother, I wasn't fit for management. What will my managers and clients say? What does this mean for me?

I run out of strength, and every step becomes heavier. I sit back on the box of paint. In one second Ethan set us back years. I have to talk to a lawyer and think about starting to separate from Ethan financially, but maybe it's too late for it now. What money do I have to protect now?

"Can you hear me, babe?" I shout to Noah through the bath-room door. "Karen's organizing a birthday party for herself. One night in the villa in April. My mom will come and look after the boys." I put his black bag on the bed and start unpacking it.

"Okay. Where's this villa?" I hear him answering through the stream of water. It's always fun when he comes home early and we can have the whole evening to ourselves. Danielle's at her mother's, and I'm peaceful and relaxed – at least until she comes back tomorrow after school.

"I have no idea. The truth is I want to get to know Tara better. She scares me a little." It's always surprised me that Karen gets along so well with her. They're so different.

"Okay," Noah replies, but I'm not sure he ever heard me.

I hang his buttoned shirts he didn't wear during his trip back in the closet and take the opportunity to check his under-wear drawer. The box is still there. I smile.

Yesterday morning I was arranging the clean laundry and saw that his drawer was completely messy. I started taking the socks out, and then I found it – a black Adler jewelry bag containing a relatively small, gift-wrapped jewelry box. I couldn't peek since it was wrapped, but I had a feeling I knew exactly what it was. To call what I felt "excitement" would be an understatement.

"I think he's about to propose to me," I immediately texted Mom, my message full of happy emojis.

She replied in one word: "Amen."

I close the drawer. What's he waiting for? If he's already bought the ring, it means he's ready to take that step. He's willing to declare it to everyone. Until I saw the box, I was desperate. I know that many couples don't get married and that it's even quite acceptable, but it's not something I ever thought would happen to me.

Noah has a kind of trauma about weddings. At my cousin's wedding a month ago, I started to cry like a little girl when I saw her father walk her down the aisle. I was excited for her, but that's not the reason I cried. I cried because I realized I'd never experience it. My parents are aging, and I always thought I would share this with them. Even now the thought of it brings tears to my eyes.

Since I unveiled this box yesterday, I can't think of anything else. It could be perfect if he proposed to me in the villa on Karen's birthday. It will probably be an amazing place, but how can I wait until then? I'll go crazy. It'd be even better if he proposes without a big production – just at home in front of Netflix. That would be good as well.

"So what's going on here at home?" Noah asks, walking out of the bathroom, still damp from his shower, wearing only underwear. When Danielle stays with us, I strongly oppose his tendency to walk around everywhere in his underwear. Now that she's not here, I have no problem with it.

"Aiden's so sweet. He's begun to draw people really well. You can even see the shape of the body. Thomas is also trying, but mostly he scribbles on Aiden's drawings, and then they start to fight, as usual." Noah sits next to me on the bed, and I show him on my phone the pictures I took of Aiden with his red hands.

"That's how brothers have fun together," Noah says.

"Oops, I almost forgot. I need to buy an amazing gift for Karen's birthday. Do you have any ideas?"

"I have no clue. Except for saying hello on the street, I don't speak to her." Noah lay on the bed and closed his eyes. "Where exactly is this event?"

"I don't know." I'm not part of the inner circle. I only know the details Karen included on the birthday's WhatsApp group. I wouldn't know what's going on without it.

This reminds me of Danielle's last birthday party. There, too, I felt like I didn't belong. Noah walked around like a star with Sarah, who looked much better than usual, and Sarah's family ignored my existence. Thomas was still a baby, and I went out to feed him in another room while Aiden remained with Noah. When I returned, I saw Sarah holding him and talking to someone, like he was her kid! She put him back on the floor the moment she saw me approaching.

"He was looking for you and you weren't here," she said in her condescending tone, "so I calmed him down."

I didn't answer. I just gave him my hand, and we went to a table that Sarah arranged for us on the far side of the room, away from her family and Noah.

"Speaking of April ... I wanted to tell you something," Noah says with his eyes closed. "I talked to Sarah today. Danielle will be staying with us for ten days in April."

A lump gets stuck in my throat, and I can hardly speak when I ask, "Ten days?"

"Yes. Sarah's travelling with her boyfriend to the Seychelles," he says, as if it's a normal thing to do.

Noah completely ignores my shock. I don't understand how I became her babysitter. I want to say, *There's no way she can stay for ten days straight*, but I remember the hidden box and take a breath. I also want to tell him about her horrible behavior when I tried to help her with the homework.

It's not the time. No. I must hold myself back. I don't want to fight with him now. He might not propose if I do, and then she'd win again. It's better to shut up. We'll deal with that when the ring's on my finger; then she'll understand exactly what's going on.

I realize that Karen's birthday is becoming even more attractive to me because it will mean two fewer days with Danielle. My mom will get along with her better than me, that's for sure, but eight days is a lot. Well, maybe with a ring it will be easier.

20

KAREN

The doctor's pills did only one thing – create sleeping problems. After a few sleepless nights, I decided to stop taking them and go back to my GP, who referred me to another neurologist. I hope that perhaps this one won't do a psychological analysis on how anxious I am. For that I have Ilene, thank you very much.

I've given up on trying to figure out what's wrong with me, and I also feel that things are a little better. Some of the numb areas feel better, and my dizziness has improved as well. My hand is still weak though. One day when I arrived early to work and was alone, I had to ask the doorman downstairs to open my Diet Coke bottle for me. It was so embarrassing, but since then he's been really nice to me and holds the door for me with a smile when I come in.

Despite my improvement, Adam said I had to keep checking, that the anxiety issue didn't seem right. This is the only reason I went to see Dr. Drew, who is new at the clinic. Now I feel anxious because I'm not sure he's experienced enough.

The clinic is in the rehabilitation wing in the hospital, and as I look around, I see people rolling around in wheelchairs, walking with crutches, and using other devices. Stressful. These patients have nothing in common with me. I'm here by mistake. Maybe I should have continued the antianxiety pills. They could have helped me a lot as I stroll through these patients.

The secretary scans the documents and sends me with a number to wait next to room 609. My heels click on the glossy floor, and I feel the stares from the people in the wheelchairs. I shrink into myself while I find a grey seat and sit down to wait. The walls are painted a boring beige, and the queue monitor broadcasts programs with healthy cooking options. I sigh. They're trying to teach me how to cook too.

I know I have something – maybe not something severe, but something. It's so frustrating that I'm exhausted all the time for no obvious reason. If I complain – God forbid – next to Ilene, she immediately scolds me. She, too, raised a child and worked as a teacher, and don't think that being a teacher is easy. It's the hardest profession. Everyone thinks it's easy to be a teacher, but that's not true. She had to work at home, even on the weekends. All that's left to me is to nod and tell her what an amazing woman she is; it's the only thing that stops her never-ending speeches.

Adam pretends he doesn't hear her, but I know her words penetrate his mind.

"Maybe that's enough already?" he asked a few days ago as soon as he came home. He probably talked to her on his way home. On the table were the leftovers from dinner, and the girls hadn't showered yet. I lay on the couch between the stacks of white and colored laundry. I asked him to come up to our room with me, and I closed the door.

"What are you doing? Do you think I want to be like that?" I asked as he unbuttoned his shirt and threw it on the bed.

"The fact is that in your office you work hard and everything's fine. It's when you're home you become sick." I saw his face, but it was Ilene's words that came out of his mouth.

"What nonsense! I have no choice at work. I can only rest at home," I replied, lying down on the bed.

"I can only rest at home too, except that I can't because when I'm back after a long day at work, I need to take care of the house." He looked at me, and I felt so small at that moment in many ways. "Maybe we need the maid for another day? Once a week isn't enough in this house," he said, emphasizing those last words.

"It's too expensive. Anyway, the second the maid leaves, the house gets dirty again from glitter or paint or chocolate."

"Then find another solution. The main thing is that something needs to change here." He left the room, and I heard him send Mia and Olivia to take a shower as he started to clean the kitchen.

When he returned to the room, I pretended to sleep, but I couldn't really fall asleep. I felt so hurt and even betrayed. He'd taken Ilene's side again – the side of the first woman in his life.

Over the past weekends, he went out with the girls to the park to ride bikes. "Mom's tired," he said, and I felt the criticism he hid from the girls.

I know I can't ride with them anymore, but I'm so disappointed. It's like I've given up on myself. I'm just afraid that one day Adam will give up on me. He wasn't too pleased with Karen Version 1.0, so what will happen now? Karen Version 2.0 is even worse.

He'll eventually replace me with a younger model. Maybe he already has someone and is just waiting for the first opportunity to escape. Maybe that's why he's looking for any opportunity for a fight, so he can say we're not getting along and that's why it has to end. He wouldn't want to be the lousy man who left a sick woman.

Adam will probably find a woman who knows how to cook

and clean, someone who even enjoys it. Like Rylie. Every time she comes to visit, she folds my laundry and picks up the toys from the floor. I really need to keep her away from my kitchen. For my birthday she'll probably bring me a family pack of bleach. That's why I hardly invite her over.

The door of room 609 opens, and a woman comes out, smiling. Maybe she knows what she has. Maybe people no longer think she's crazy or anxious. Maybe she's not imagining hidden illnesses that aren't discovered by any means just to avoid the laundry. I don't know whether to enter the room or wait.

"Karen, you can come in."

I close the door behind me and place on the table the binder that I brought with all the tests I've already had done. With the face of a teenager, Dr. Drew looks younger than me in his blue buttoned shirt. I was expecting a kind of fatherly figure, a medical expert to take my medical mystery and lead me to the long-awaited diagnosis, someone experienced and reassuring who will bring me back to my old self. I don't have the energy to be a guinea pig for a young doctor who doesn't know where and what he's looking for exactly.

Dr. Drew types fast, recording everything I tell him, which is also indicative of his youth. Older doctors type with one finger. The room is very different from our high-tech work environment. It holds a white desk with a computer and two seats for the patient and their companion, and, of course, a bed covered with cheap paper that's being replaced (hopefully) between patients.

I tell him everything that's happened over the past year, from the dizziness to the numbness of my hand. "I'm sorry. I hate it that I sound like some miserable old woman. It's just hard for me," I say, not letting myself cry. I'm afraid the crying will make him give me tranquilizers and send me home, like the previous neurologist.

"That's fine. The details are helpful, so we won't miss

anything. I'm referring you to all sorts of tests. Come back to me with all the results when you have them," he says, and for the first time, I feel that the doctor in front of me believes me. "Even if we don't find exactly what's wrong, I believe we can help your fatigue and your pain with medication."

I walk out of the clinic a little calmer. I found someone who doesn't think I should be hospitalized here in the psychiatric ward. I have hope again that they'll find something to prove that my complaints are real – not that I really want them to find something. I just want to bring Ilene a letter that proves my complaints were justified. I want to finally have sharp, solid, conclusive evidence. That's all.

On the way to the parking lot, I glance at the list of tests. Three MRIs. When exactly will I find time for all these tests?

Today's my long day at work, and Ilene and Jacob will pick up the girls from school. I decide to call and make all the appointments in the afternoon when there are fewer people in the office. My team must believe that I'm tough and strong. I don't want them to know because they'll start fighting about who will replace me. I've already noticed that Anna walks around Will's office every chance she has and glorifies herself. She's just waiting for the opportunity, and I can't let her smell blood.

When only Dave and his big headphones remain in the aquarium, I start to make my calls, setting the appointments for all three MRIs in the middle of the night. That way the girls won't see me go, and no one will know about it at work. An excellent solution.

I didn't say anything to Tara about the appointment today either. I've seen the faces she makes as I complain about something, the way she raises her perfect eyebrows (which cost her quite a bit) and looks at me patronizingly. Rylie could be an advertisement for health, so what would she understand about living in my body?

Although there are still a few weeks until my tests, I send my brother the dates and ask him to accompany me. He's not working, and it's better that Adam stays home with the girls. I can't ask Jacob and Ilene to come in the middle of the night – Ilene would never, ever forget it. Even when I gave birth to Amelia and called her to come at night to stay with Mia and Olivia, she complained for months and claimed I deliberately gave birth the night before her choir concert. Unbelievable.

When Adam doesn't feel well, he goes to bed and doesn't leave until he recovers. Ilene is ready to come every hour to bring him chicken soup, and if she sees me asking him for help with something, she scolds me for being selfish and not taking care of her sick son. It's only I who must function with all this pain, as if nothing's going on with me. These are the moments when I miss my parents in the most painful way imaginable.

As the evening goes on, I feel more and more tired. Dave's working hard, and I'm wandering a bit on Facebook, looking for recommendations for all kinds of activities we can do on my birthday. Everything's so expensive, though, and we also have the costs of the villa.

I'm supposed to end up going through the changes Anna made on the website, but I can't concentrate. I decide to get up to make myself a cup of coffee. Maybe that will help me recover a little ...

I open my eyes.

I'm lying on the floor of the office, and Dave is standing in front of me, the white headphones on his ears, lifting my legs up.

My head really aches, and I faintly hear him ask, "Karen, are you okay?"

21

TARA

"Don't you think you should get up already?" I ask Ethan as I put on my shoes and open the door of our bedroom.

"Leave me alone," he grumbles to the pillow, covering his head with a blanket, defending himself against the light coming in. Hiding from the world like a spoiled teenager.

I look at him lying there, his belly peeking out of the blanket, and I try to remember where the handsome man I once loved disappeared to, the one who approached me at a beach party.

It was too many years ago. Ethan was wearing tight jeans and a black shirt, which was tight from his muscles back then, not from the beer. He started dancing next to me, a little too close, and my friend whispered, "I think he wants some attention."

I turned to him and danced, and occasionally he tried to reach out. I braked it with sharp movements. When the party was over, he shoved a note into my hand with his phone number like we were part of some sticky advertisement. I threw it in the bin and moved on with my life. I found out later that my friend gave him my number, and after a few days, he called.

Something intrigued me about him at first. He talked about how much money he would make and threw around names of all sorts of famous people. He made me feel like he was a man of the world, and I believed that together we could conquer the world. We saw a lot of the world together – far more than I thought I'd see and much more than my parents ever did.

Ethan also liked going out to clubs. He liked the noise, music, cigarettes of all kinds, and lots of drunk and sticky people. It's incredible that I once enjoyed such outings too. Unfortunately, he still enjoys it, and I've grown older in the meantime. I was that dumb girl who thought that someday something would change, that he would become a father and change his behavior. The fact is that I have five children, and Juvi and I raise them together.

He turns over in bed and snores.

"Idiot," I say quietly so the kids won't hear, wanting to send him to his mom so she can deal with the rebel boy. Instead, I walk out of the room nervously and close the door behind me.

"Good morning." Juvi greets me with a smile and hands me my red thermal glass. I decided to make my coffee at home – at least until we get settled in the new offices.

"Good morning, Juvi," I say, but I can't bring myself to smile. I'm tired after another sleepless night. I argued with Ethan until one in the morning, and then I couldn't fall asleep. I just lay in bed thinking what to do, how to get out of this mess, wondering if maybe some of the money can be saved. Ethan, on the other hand, slept great.

Juvi continues to smile. God knows what I would do without her. I would definitely lose my mind. When I get home in the evening, the kids are usually clean and ready for bed, whereas if Ethan's home, he just gets in the way. I don't have a clue how mothers get along without an au pair. I know I can't.

I pass the mirror at the entrance and see an old, worn-out woman looking at me, a woman for whom no amount of makeup can help. The concealer can't hide the black circles either. My necklace with the red glass squares does add some color and stands out against the black silk shirt, but my eyes don't lie. They show the signs of the last several nights.

"Mom, are you taking us?" Mason asks impatiently. Ella's ready with her bag, with the enthusiasm that only a first-grader can have.

"Sure, my love." I take the keys with a smile. I hate the queue at drop-off, where the cars are waiting to unload children, but today it might be good for me to arrive later at the bank. Maybe some of the problems will work out by themselves.

On the way to school, the kids are quiet, and I think that it would be nice to drop them off at school and go back home. Instead, I have to start another crazy day handling challenges and complaints and customers who always want more than you can offer them (and if they don't get what they want, they threaten to move to another bank), and employees who want to work less.

Then I remember Ethan not moving his ass out of bed. I remember the lies he told me. I can't believe a word that comes out of his mouth, and I'm sure he didn't see any document. He just gave the money to Alex. Just like that. Like an idiot. And he still blames me for being hysterical. I'd rather go to the bank and handle other people's messes than my own. I don't want to go back home to Ethan.

On the sidewalk I see Rylie running with someone on the street. She's probably giving a private training. She's wearing Adidas sports tights and a matching tight tank top that show off her perfect body. She looks like an advertisement for Adidas. Even lazy Ethan would be willing to run after a girl like Rylie.

At the school entrance, the kids jump out of the Jeep before I even stop properly. They slam the door behind them and run.

How I would like to go to the ocean now, to sit in front of

the water with a glass of wine and just stare at the water with no purpose. And breathe.

I would like to breathe.

On the way to the bank, I can't stop myself from thinking about how to get out of this mess. Ethan's certainly not part of the solution. I can't lose all our savings because of his nonsense.

I decide to talk to Adam and see if maybe he can help or if he knows someone who can. When I call, I discover that he, too, is stuck in traffic on his way to his office. After I explain to him why I'm calling, he asks, "Do you have any other assets other than your house?"

"Shared? Only the house and the savings. Ahh, and there's the house I inherited from my dad. Is that considered common?"

"No. Basically, it's yours. What exactly have you got there?" Adam asks.

"I inherited my dad's part in my parents' house. My mother lives there. It's not in my name yet, but I did get his will approved."

"Then consider the possibility of selling the property if you need access to any available money," Adam says, not realizing it means opening another front with my mom, the unofficial president of Ethan's fan club. "Regarding the funds at the trustee, give me a few days to check and I'll be in touch."

After the initial shock, I understand that Adam might be right, and selling my parent's house is a real option. The house is worth a lot of money, and it's too big for my mom. She can move to a smaller apartment. Financially, this money will give me the security I need, and if Ethan has no part in it, that's amazing. I just need to sell house after we separate. Unfortunately, right now it's only theory.

The situation is much more complex than financial calculations. Selling Mom's home isn't another real estate transaction.

This is the house that holds so many memories with my dad – family dinners, that time I told him I got my first job at the bank, the first time he saw Mason, the only child of mine he met.

The house hasn't changed much since he died. The walls are full of pictures – my mother's wall of fame. Even my wedding picture with Ethan in a tacky gold frame hangs next to the pictures of my sisters' weddings. At each wedding, we used to take a family picture of us all, and they all hang around the pictures of the happy couple. On the wall hangs pictures of the grandchildren of all ages, from birth to graduation.

I wonder what the protocol is for the wall of fame in case of a divorce. This hasn't happened in our family yet. Maybe we should remove all pictures of the divorcee? Maybe they just blacken the divorcee's face in the shared pictures?

My mom refused my sister's offer to move in close to her, claiming that she's comfortable in her own home. She smokes on the porch with her friends when they come over twice a week to play cards, she grows her mint in big brown molds, she cooks for the grandchildren who come for a visit or stay for the weekends. And, of course, she cooks for Ethan. She isn't as young as she thinks she is, and moving her to another place will not be easy.

It's hard to give up on all those memories because of Ethan. I'm so mad at him when I think of it. Without a doubt, selling should be the final act, but if Adam doesn't find another solution, I might not have a choice. In the meantime, I should make sure my part of the house is registered under my name.

The question is how to do it without my mother finding out. If I tell her, she might tell Ethan. They have a lot of conversations about how hard he works and how poor he is.

That's right, Mom. Poor Ethan.

22

RYLIE

"I cursed you for two days after the last workout," Jenny tells me with a smile at the end of her workout. "I can barely climb the stairs. My muscles are still sore."

"Great. It means you're doing something right. Make sure to get your stomach in and work those pelvic-floor muscles."

Women who hear "pelvic-floor" are straining more. I've learned that the fear of uterine prolapse gives them a lot of motivation.

Jenny comes out, and I set up the studio. The kids are still in the middle of their shower, and judging by the enthusiasm I hear, Mom will probably get out of there wet to the bones. Danielle is closed in her room, as usual. At least she doesn't get in the way. I imagine her sitting on her bed and eating her candies, and I wonder where she hides the wrappers. Conniving little monster.

"I'm out for a run," I shout to Mom. "I'll be back in an hour."

"No problem, honey," Mom replies through the children's cheers. They don't even care where I'm going because she bought them bath paints. *Good luck getting them out of the bath.*

I haven't found time to run during the last week. Thomas

was sick, followed by Aiden, and I feel like my body has already degenerated. I get out of the house and play the music I love, noticing that Tara's house is all lit up. I see her through the window with Emma in her hands. I'd never get along with four children. I barely make it with two. Without Mom, I'd go crazy.

I still hope that my third, if there is a third, will be a girl – but not like Danielle. I want a normal, nice, smiling daughter. Like Karen's daughters.

"I didn't think it mattered much, three or four, but as it turns out, this whole baby phase is tiring," Tara once told me. "You'll see when you get older," she added with a smile, reminding me (again) that I'm younger than her.

I pass by the school and hear noise coming from the basketball court. It's nice to hear the women screaming enthusiastically. Women's basketball is going strong lately, and I even considered joining the team, but I've always preferred running. It allows me to be with myself and think, especially since the birth of Aiden.

Coldplay's new song has barely started when it's immediately replaced by the ring of my phone. A picture of me kissing Mom last year appears on the screen. I only left forty minutes ago. Why is she calling?

"What's going on, Mommy?" I answer, panting, but keeping my stride. "Is everything okay?"

"Yes, everything's fine now, but you have to come back." She sounds nervous, which is unlike her. I'm really worried now, almost hysterical.

"What's wrong? Are the kids okay?" I turn around and head back home.

"It's Thomas," she replies, and I notice her voice is trembling. "He's fine now, but he choked."

"Oh my God! I'm coming!" I hang up and start running home as fast as I can, probably breaking a world record. "It's okay," I tell myself over and over again out loud, as if it will help me relax. "She said he was okay."

I quickly climb the stairs, dripping with sweat, but it's unclear if it's due to my effort or the pressure and worry I feel. The door is open, and Mom is at the entrance with Thomas in her hands. He seems fine. Thank God. He is fine.

"He's okay, honey," Mom says as Thomas throws himself toward me. His amazing eyes are red from crying, and I can see that Mom is still shaking, so I hug her with my other hand.

"What happened to him?" I look at Mom, giving her a few seconds to speak.

"I'm really sorry, honey. It was an accident," she says with a trembling voice as tears leak from her eyes. "I was putting away the dishes, and for a second I turned my back. He probably took an apple from the bowl." She points toward the fruit bowl on the dining table. "It all happened so fast. He began to cough and made scary noises. He turned blue, and he was holding the apple. I didn't know what to do. I—"

"It's okay, Mommy." I hug her, and her tears continue. "He's fine now." I keep my arm wrapped around her, and we enter the house together.

Only then I get it, and I'm shocked. Aiden is sitting on Danielle's lap, and they're watching *PAW Patrol* together. He explains something to her, and she nods and smiles at him. It's a total shock. Then he puts his head on her, and they sit like this together.

"What's going on here?" I ask Mom quietly.

"You won't believe how lucky we were that Danielle was here. I didn't know what to do. He choked and I banged him on his back over and over and nothing came out. Danielle heard me scream and came downstairs. She picked him up and did something – I don't know what she did – but the piece of apple just flew out of his mouth."

"Really?"

Danielle? I think. *Are we talking about the same girl? The girl who wasn't even ready to say hello to Aiden and who never held Thomas in her hands?*

Mom nods and wipes her face with a tissue.

"Danielle, do you know first aid?" I put Thomas down, and he runs to Mom as I sit next to them on the couch and Aiden smiles at me.

"Yes. I mean, we've learned in school," she says, continuing to look at the puppies rescuing a warehouse, as if she doesn't want to lose even a second of the episode. "They explained to us what to do if a baby suffocates."

"I can't believe it. Thank you!" I look at her, but she doesn't look at me. "Thank you so much, Danielle. How lucky you were here," I say, and I can't believe those words come out of my mouth. I really want to hug her, but I don't know how she'll react, so I just sit there.

"It's not a big deal," she replies still looking at the screen. I notice that she gently strokes Aiden's hand, and he seems to be trying not to move it.

"Thank you. I really mean it. You're a life saver." I turn to reassure Mom, who is in the kitchen walking in circles with Thomas. She doesn't stop muttering to herself and kissing him.

I realize this is the first time Danielle and I have actually spoken to each other. No anger. No shouts. It's the first time that I felt a positive emotion toward her. As I get up and hug Mommy, I look at Danielle sitting with Aiden and feel like she's someone I never met before. Maybe it's the smile. I think I see dimples. But I also see something else in her eyes as she looks at Aiden, something that's starting to resemble the look she has when she sees Noah.

Mom went home, and the boys fell asleep. Noah's not home yet, so I get into bed, wanting to watch an episode on Netflix until Noah comes back, but I can't concentrate on anything. Whenever I remember what happened to Thomas, I feel my pulse rise and the adrenaline rush. It's hard for me to relax. What a disaster it could have been for us. I would never have believed that Danielle would do something like that. I must admit – if only to myself – that Danielle seems a little less monstrous to me now.

I get out of bed and go into the hallway, standing in front of Danielle's closed door. The "Keep Out" sign is already loosening from all the door slams. I'm not sure whether to enter her room or not. I don't really know what to say to her.

"You can't believe what happened today!" I hear her say and move closer to the door to try to hear better. "My little brother choked on an apple. She was running, so I performed the Heimlich maneuver on him. I swear." I've never heard her call one of the boys a "brother" before. "Obviously," Danielle continues, "she'll probably tell my dad too."

She says a few things that I can't hear, but I continue to stand there quietly.

"I've already told you. No way." I realize that she's probably talking about something else, and I start to move away from her door when I hear her say, "Do you think I'll tell somebody? Are you crazy? Snitching's the worst. That bitch will kill me."

23

KAREN

In the weeks following the famous faint, I actually feel an improvement. Will, the CEO, asks me constantly how I'm doing, so I try to act as if nothing's wrong with me, as if I feel great. Every time I see him, I try to look happy and energetic, even though it's eight in the evening. I tell him about the team's achievements, sometimes with a bit exaggeration, and I never complain. Never.

I went back to exercise at Rylie's, and I feel less tired. It seems the vitamin supplements Ilene gave me have helped. Even my blurred vision and the pain in my legs are gone. The numbness remains the same, but I've gotten used to it. It's been less disturbing, and I feel a little bit more like myself.

Adam is also less nervous and less anxious since things have improved and I've begun to function as before. For Ilene, of course, that's not good enough, but that's not something that time can cure. She undoubtedly suffers from a phenomenon called "chronic dissatisfaction."

It takes me a while to decide whether to go for all the tests that Dr. Drew ordered for me, but eventually I decide to go. It's better to be calm and rule out all the bad things, just to be on the safe side and be sure. I must put the frightening options aside and move forward. I recently even considered changing my diet, which probably wouldn't hurt. Rylie suggested I attend a detoxification workshop that's supposed to help in cases of fatigue, but I don't see myself drinking squeezed juices. It would be a waste of money and time.

Steven and I drive at night for the last MRI, exhausted from the previous late-night drives to the hospital. We take advantage of the shared time and bring up funny memories of our parents. Walking down the abandoned, half-dark corridors of the hospital, we laugh all the way to the imaging center.

"These are the results from your first scan," the receptionist tells me, placing a page in front of me with the results of my head scan.

Maybe it's because it comes after a long period of complaints that no one took seriously, or maybe it's because I'm tired of sleepless nights, but when I see what's written there, I just burst into uncontrollable laughter.

In black and white, it's written right there: the findings match multiple sclerosis. I feel pure happiness, as if I've just been informed that I won a luxurious weekend. That's how happy I am.

"Are you crazy? These are really bad results." Steven looks at me from above, probably embarrassed by the noise I'm making. The people in the waiting room look at me in pity.

"On the contrary, now I know I'm not crazy. Something is actually wrong! I didn't imagine it all." I'm so excited that the receptionist is asking me to be a little quieter, but I feel like dancing in the hallway with joy. If I were up to opening a front with Ilene, I'd call her now and tell her, "I told you so!" I think I should frame the results and hang them in the living room.

I take a picture of the results and send it to Adam, who is waiting for me at home. He immediately replies, "What does that mean?"

"That means I was right!" I answer, but he doesn't respond. He probably doesn't know what to say.

Steven takes me home, and before I leave the car, he says, "I'm sorry you're sick." I open the door in the semi-dark street, and he adds, "You really don't deserve it."

"Thank you, little brother." The door slams and it's loud in the empty street. The sun's already rising, and the sky begins to clear. I sneak home quietly, like the nights after releasing a new version, except that this time I'm returning with very serious bugs that I have no way to fix.

The place where the contrast was injected hurts, and I curse quietly as I take off the bandage they applied in the hospital. I undress and curl up in my blanket. Adam's asleep, and I hear his deep breaths, jealous of his ability to fall asleep in any situation. I close my eyes and try to understand what it all means.

It's not good news, but at least I know I'm not crazy. The noisy thoughts fly all over my head until I give up and unlock my phone. I Google "MS" and read the articles: disability, pain, memory problems, bladder problems. Oh my God, what awaits me? The joy of discovery is replaced by fear. What will happen in the future? Will I have a wheelchair? A walker? A Filipino to take care of me? I've been feeling a lot better recently, so how does that make sense?

When will the next relapse occur? What damages will it leave? This illness is unexpected, and it's unclear what starts it and what makes it progress. I read that stress can cause relapses, and I realize that it started when we were working like crazy on that big project. I didn't sleep and just thought of code lines day and night. Add to this the mess at home and the girls and you'll find stress. Apparently, it's no coincidence that there are more women with MS than men. We take on too much.

I read more and more, and tears wet my pillow. At some point, I'm exhausted enough to fall asleep.

Adam's alarm clock wakes me too soon. When Adam goes

into the shower, I lie down, trying to remember what I'm supposed to do today and why I'm still in bed. The recognition comes back with the harsh feeling of the diagnosis I got last night.

I hide underneath the blanket, and Adam sits down next to me. "Do you need help with something? Do you want me to stay with you today?"

"NO. There's no need for you to stay." Nothing's changed since yesterday. *Yesterday, I had MS, and you didn't offer to stay and help.* I look at him, trying to catch his eyes, but he looks away and ties his shoelaces. *What if one day I'm not able to tie my laces? Will you help me or tell me I'm pampered?*

"Okay. I'll take the girls so you can get some rest." Adam walks out of the room quietly, and I hear him wake up the girls.

I had planned in advance to arrive late for work, but I decide not to go at all. I don't want to see anyone today. I need time for myself, time to regroup. I text Will that I'm sick and staying home.

I have so many things I need to understand, not only learning about this disease, but also how I'm going to deal with it. I know it's a mistake, but I Google again. This time I read more carefully, going through the existing treatments and everything I find related to the subject.

On Facebook, I look for relevant groups and join some of them. In tears, I answer "yes" to the question, "Do you have MS?"

Unread messages begin to fill my WhatsApp in all sorts of groups, and Adam reminds me of his existence by sending me a surprising text: "If you need something, call me."

I continue to cry in bed and silence my phone. The smell of Ethan's cigarettes comes in through the window, and I close it tightly. I really don't want to get sick from passive smoking as well.

Even in recent weeks, despite the slight improvement in our

relationship, there has been a certain tension between Adam and me. I've had to deal with the physical difficulties and continue to act normal with the girls and at work, without any support. Throughout this period, the only thing I got from my environment was criticism. How much longer can I go on like this?

I want to call Tara and tell her, "I told you something was wrong." I want to prove to the world that I was right, but I regret those thoughts quickly. Maybe it's better that no one knows. Maybe people won't understand what it is, and they'll stay away from me, pity me. I need friends, not mercy.

I text Daria "Hi," but she's still sleeping in Boston, and her moving away feels even worse. Daria was more down to earth, and we were so close. Although I've gotten closer to Tara, our relationship is a little odd to me. Her life is so different from mine. Her dilemmas are whether to buy Ethan a new watch or just a small yacht as a gift. They're the neighborhood Kardashians. I'm totally happy for them, but can she understand my life? How can she understand what it's like to live with a serious illness?

They keep calling from the office all morning. A malfunction has disabled one of the servers. As soon as he discovered it, Will texted me, asking if I was sure I couldn't come, if only for a few hours. For the first time ever, I replied, "I can't. Sorry."

I don't know what tomorrow will bring and how I'll get up in the morning. Every day I can have a new flare-up – just like that, out of the blue. I have to make an effort and continue to function normally as long as possible, but I'm allowed to take one day for myself. To grieve a little, get angry, cry.

Tomorrow I'll be strong again. But not today.

If they find out about the disease at work, I'll be out the door within five minutes, and who will hire me afterward? How will I go to all the checkups? Each one will cost me at least half a working day. Will might consider transferring me to another position, as if to help me. He'll be afraid to trust me with his bigger projects, so he'll give me less-important clients and maybe take me off the management team. Anna will be the head of the team. She's just waiting for it.

I don't want them to know in the neighborhood either, since I don't want the girls to find out. They don't need to live in fear. If Mia hears the name of the disease, she'll immediately check her phone and know everything. No. It's better not to tell anyone for now.

In two months I'll celebrate my birthday as everything is settled. I decided to book a luxurious villa with a pool for one night. Am I allowed to use a pool? I check and see that it's not written anywhere that it's forbidden. I don't feel like organizing this party at all. From now on, everything will be worse. What exactly do I have to celebrate?

Just before noon I get out of bed and look for something sweet to eat. There's nothing in the house. I must go shopping for Nutella and, most importantly, to get ready for the girls. I should get cereals and a carton of milk as well.

Anna's name appears on the screen again. I answer, and she updates me that the problem's been fixed. She starts to whine about breaking up with her boyfriend after two years. She expected him to pull out a ring – not the key to her apartment. I try to listen and find a little empathy in my heart, but I feel drained. Completely blocked. As if my container is empty of feelings for anyone but myself. I no longer have room for other people's problems, certainly not for stupid ones. Another guy will come. Maybe she'll even finally find her Adam. It's not like she's going to be a disabled person in a wheelchair, right?

24

TARA

"Mom! Mom!" Ella calls me from her room.

"What do you need, my love?" I sit down next to her and gently stroke her soft hair, which clings to her forehead.

"Why is Dad at home all day? Is he sick?" I can see her concern in her brown eyes. This little girl has such a big heart.

"No, my love. He just took some time off work," I reply. "It's fun to have him home, isn't it?"

"He watches TV all the time. He doesn't play with us at all." Her sad eyes squeeze my heart.

"He's resting, darling. When he finishes resting, he will play with you all the time." I give her millions of little kisses, and she laughs. "Now go to bed, it's very late." I tighten the blanket around her and leave the room.

Walking into my bedroom, I find Ethan watching another football game. Mixed feelings of anger, disgust, and disappointment flood me, mingle, and create a fierce sense of hatred. Sex hasn't been a part of our relationship for months now. As I examine the room, the empty plates lying on the floor by the bed are the only change I see from the morning. He's hiding here like a mouse. Poor Juvi must have been afraid to come in here.

"Your daughter's worried about you," I say.

Ethan continues to stare at the screen. "What do you want from me? You just came back and you already want a fight?"

"You haven't gone out for weeks now. Don't you think you've gotten carried away about all this?"

"How will I look my employees in the eye? What am I supposed to tell them? Everyone knows I'm invested with Alex. What do you want me to do?" He lies on the bed with his hairy belly peering out between yesterday's shirt and his pants. He surfs through all the sports channels we have in our expanded package, and almost all of them feature someone kicking a ball. I want to kick Ethan out of the house.

"What do I want you to do? There's a price for your adventures and now we both must pay it. Tell them you were an idiot who lost all your children's savings on a fictitious deal. That's what you tell them."

"Leave me alone."

I begin to imagine myself without him at home and can't find a lot of differences, but first, we need to solve this problem of him lying in bed all day. Ethan must go to work and bring some money home. I'm trying to get the money from the trustee. I recall the lawyer's recommendations; a few days ago, this discussion was theoretical. Now it's real. I almost forgot about this meeting because of all the pressure I'm under at the bank and at home.

I started the process of moving my part in Mom's house to my name as Adam suggested. I must have something, some base of my own, something Ethan can't touch. I contacted Adam, and he arranged for someone in his office to take over the transfer of ownership, but I haven't told anyone – not my mother nor my sisters. I don't need any more wars right now. Adam has also checked on our legal status with the trustee.

"So what exactly is your plan?" I sit down on the bed, trying to be as calm as I can.

"I don't know," he replies.

That's exactly your problem, you idiot, I think to myself, trying to keep calm. "Look, there's no point in staying home. Go back to work and earn some money. The business isn't the same if you're not there, right?"

"I don't know."

This conversation is going nowhere. Every passing day just brings us down even more. His secretary has already called me several times because he missed important meetings, and I didn't know what to tell her. I felt like the mother of a schoolboy when the teacher phones to tell her that her boy is failing at school.

I take the remote and turn off the TV.

"What are you doing?" he shouts, and this time he even looks in my direction.

"I want you to listen to me and listen carefully. Tomorrow you will get up in the morning and go to your car dealership and that's it. It's time to stop this nonsense," I say resolutely.

"Leave me already!" he yells and then goes into the shower, closing the door behind him.

"You have to pull yourself together. Look for a lawyer and try to get the money back. But in the meantime, go to work!" I say to the closed door, knowing he hears me.

"We'll see. Just shut up."

"Don't you realize that everything you do affects the whole family? You have four children here. Four! You don't live in a vacuum. You lost all our savings because of this Alex, and now I have to do everything on my own."

"Did someone tell you to do something? I'll handle it!"

"How will you handle it exactly? Please tell me. I'm listening." I try hard to lower my voice.

"I told you I'm taking care of it, so that's enough. You're not my mother. Leave me alone!"

I hear Ethan flush, and then when he gets out of the shower, he goes back to bed. The game goes on, and he turns up the volume. I understand that there's no one to talk to, and the truth is, I can't believe a word he says – I couldn't even before the story with Alex. After all that's happened, even if he tells me that the sun is out, I'll open a window to check for myself.

It's my turn to escape to the bathroom. I look in the mirror and feel like I've aged years during the last weeks. My hair needs coloring – preferably before Karen's birthday. This is not the look I want perpetuated in photos, and certainly not on Instagram.

I check my mobile. It's almost ten o'clock. I've missed many texts on the birthday group.

"What do you say about a stylist as an activity at the party?" Karen asked about an hour ago.

"Sounds great," Rylie replied, "but whatever you want."

"I'm happy with everything," I write, but I have no desire to think about the birthday. That's all Karen's been talking about lately. If I ask how she is, she answers with something about the birthday plans, as if it's the only thing happening in the world right now – Karen turning forty. It's unbelievable that there are people who can get so involved in organizing parties and have no real concern for anyone or anything else. If she has any idea how to reprogram Ethan's brain, though, I'm ready to listen.

Rylie types: "Do we need to bring groceries for dinner?"

"You don't need anything. Just be there by five," Karen answers.

What's she doing awake at such an hour? She's usually in bed by nine. Whenever I ask if she's free to go out for a glass of wine, she says she's tired.

I place the phone on the wooden surface next to the sink,

and tired eyes look at me from the mirror. I take off my necklace and put it in the drawer. I hear another beep. I need to silence this group.

From the bedroom, I hear Ethan screaming at the TV as if the players can hear him. Maybe I should send him to art therapy with Mason since Mason's teacher has recommended that I take him. She also gave me the name of someone she recommended, but I haven't dealt with it yet.

Ethan could tell the therapist how unfortunate he is, and then he could draw a tree for her.

A tree that grows money.

25

KAREN

A few days after the last MRI test, Adam and I met with Dr. Drew and got the final confirmation: I have MS. I knew he didn't have any rabbit he could pull out of his hat to make reality easier. We left with instructions for me to rest more and start to inject myself three times a week with a medicine that's supposed to stop the progression of the disease.

"Everything else is luck," he said, and I thought that good luck isn't common in my family.

"Don't say anything to anyone," I told Adam on the way to the parking lot. "Not to your parents either. We'll continue as usual."

"Whatever you want." Adam held my hand, and we walked slowly, stealing more time for ourselves. It had been hard for him to look me in the eye lately, but at least there was intimacy between us again.

"Do you think I should say something at work?"

"You don't have to say anything yet. If there's a problem, we'll solve it," he told me, and I liked his decisive tone.

Adam reassured me, but I had a feeling that he didn't fully understand what I was going through. He hadn't sat for hours and consulted Dr. Google. He hadn't read the articles about the problems with sexual function. He continued to live his life as usual. This disease is just theoretical for him, and his lack of involvement in the details has left me to deal with the fear of the future alone.

It's true that he's been trying more lately. Since the diagnosis, he's much more patient and does things at home without complaining. He asks me how I feel ten times a day and brings me things I like to eat. When Ilene asked him why there was laundry in the living room again while I rested in bed, he asked her, in a determined voice, to stop it. For the first time since we got married, he stood up against her. I was shocked. It was a miracle, and all that was needed was a chronic disease.

Since graduating, my dream job has been to be a head of a development team. I knew that if I had this line on my CV, it would be easy for me to move to another company in the future. I was on the right track, and it was all going well – until this illness came along. Now I'm not performing well at work. It's hard for me to endure the long hours, and when I get home, I immediately get back into bed, barely able to spend time with the girls.

Lately, the stress I have at work – fixings crashing websites in the middle of the night, being available to customers 24/7, always being nice and patient with their nonsense – is too much for me. I feel like I can't cope with this stress at work along with this illness. On top of it all, I have to deal with the side effects of the injections. It's just too much for me.

The only thing I can do lately is work and go for all the tests Dr. Drew sends me to do. Everything else just doesn't happen. It's not the life I thought I would have. In the morning after the injection I feel like I've got the flu. My body hurts, and I feel so weak. That's how I feel every other day, and with great difficulty, I take Advil and drag myself to work.

Tara told me yesterday that she was exhausted because

Emma woke her up at night. I didn't want to whine, so I just told her it was really annoying and hopefully the next night would be easier. Inside, though, I wanted to tell her that I felt that all the time, even without being woken every hour. That's how I live, day after day – exhausted, as if I have permanent jet lag but without the fun of traveling abroad.

I didn't want this illness to change my life. I didn't want to give in to it, but I can see that as the weeks pass, it's getting harder. I have a hard time working on the computer. The fatigue, the pain, and the visual difficulties are getting worse. It happened gradually, so I didn't notice it at first, but I feel I'm about to give up. The treatment makes me feel even sicker, and I can't continue to live as if nothing's wrong. It's just not working for me anymore.

I've already told Rylie that if I can make it to the workout, I'll let her know. She shouldn't count on me. I can no longer function in the evening like I used to, and come to think of it, I can't in the morning either. I'm losing patience with my employees and with some of the more demanding clients as well. I come home and just wait for Adam to come back and rescue me.

"Stop that noise," I shouted earlier to Mia, who was doing a new Tik-Tok video with Olivia. "I can't stand it anymore!"

"Then go to your room," Mia said and continued with the awful music.

"Don't be rude! Go upstairs!" I screamed at her. "And bring me your phone. I'll hold on to it until tomorrow!"

"Why? What did I do? You're just a horrible mother! The worst mother in the world!" Mia threw her phone on the couch, stamped her way to her room, and slammed the door.

Olivia and Lia looked at me in disbelief. I turned the television on to the Disney channel and sent Adam a message with shaking hands: "Please come home now."

When Adam finally comes home, he opens the door and finds me lying in bed, crying with guilt in the dark.

"I can't do it anymore," I murmur. "I'm sick of it all."

"Everything will be fine. Dr. Drew said it takes time to balance the medication." Adam sits down next to me and gently pats my head. "Maybe you should take some days off from work."

"It won't help!" I continue to cry on my pillow, feeling like a little girl crying for her dad. "I come home exhausted and I take it all out on the girls. I use up all the energy I have at work."

"What do you want to do?"

"I want to get out of the race," I say, surprising myself. "I'll set up a freelance business and work from home for a while. No stress. No CEO hovering over me. No employees. Just me."

"Okay then. I don't see a problem with your plans. We'll talk to my accountant and see what needs to be done."

"Really?" I sit up, and for a moment I feel new hope.

"Really." Adam smiles, kissing my wet face.

I hug him tight, like a princess hugging the knight who rescued her from a haunted castle.

"I must tell you something," Adam says after a few minutes of silence. "Do you remember Alex, the client who didn't pay me my fees?" Adam lets go of the hug, and I lie back down.

"Ethan's friend?"

"Yes. It turns out the police have arrested him on charges of fake real estate deals. He's under house arrest. That explains why he's not answering our calls." Adam unbuttons his shirt and puts it in the laundry basket. It took me years to get him to put it straight there and not just throw it on the chair.

"Wow. How shocking. Was your office involved in those deals?"

"Definitely not. Apparently, he had another lawyer who took care of it, thank God. He threw Alex out and then he came to me. I just prepared two letters for him. That's it."

"How lucky," I say quietly, thinking of Tara.

I wonder what she knows about it. She surely knows something. It's so strange that she didn't say anything to me. I saw her earlier today when we picked up the kids from school. She usually has such a big smile on her face, a smile that lights up the room, but not today. Today she seemed upset. Alex is probably the reason for that.

"Two police officers arrived today to make copies of his files. They asked a few questions and left. I think I was miraculously saved from a huge legal mess." Adam lies down next to me.

"Please don't accept clients from Ethan anymore. It's not worth it."

"That's for sure."

Olivia calls Adam, and he goes out to her while I stay in the room. Maybe Ethan is also connected to these fake deals? It's nice to have other things to think about that aren't my problems. I haven't talked much to Tara about Ethan's work, but when I showed some interest, she responded by dismissing me.

Tara never talks much about him. I know he has a car dealership and that he doesn't handle real estate. Ethan constantly flies abroad and looks busy and successful. Occasionally I see his check-in on Facebook, every time in another fancy hotel in another country.

They always seemed like a perfect couple to me, travelling all the time, living a good life. She's like the perfect woman – an exemplary career woman who is raising four children and even knows how to cook properly. Grandma Ilene's perfect daughter-in-law.

Now that I know Tara better, I don't know why she married Ethan in the first place. They're so different. She's much more intelligent than him, and more successful and talented. She got promoted in her own right at the bank. It's kind of a success story in the masculine financial world.

Ethan always talks as if he knows everything, but after one

or two questions, one can see that he's just a hollow person. There's nothing to him except luxury watches and big cars, and there's nothing particularly promising under this hat of his. He always struts around like a peacock, pleased with himself for no real reason. How does Tara get along with him at all?

What will Tara say when she finds out that I quit my job? She always told me she didn't appreciate women who didn't work, that every woman should be independent and make money for herself. I would have to tell her, but I'd have to present it in a way that wouldn't cause her to suspect that something was wrong with me. Maybe I can present it as if I decided to change my life as a part of my fortieth birthday resolution. As something good. A new beginning. Not as my failure in dealing with this illness that struck me.

At some point I fall asleep, and by the time I wake up in the morning, I have an excellent sentence for everyone around me: I'm leaving my job to start a new business.

I take a painkiller and go to the office to give Will my resignation.

26

RYLIE

My box is still in the drawer, hiding among Noah's ironed underwear. I checked this morning again after he left for work, dressed in jeans and a T-shirt as is customary in start-up companies. For meetings, he dresses more formally, but only from the waist up since they're usually video conferences.

I haven't told him I saw the box. I don't want to ruin his plans. I know it can't disappear, but I check several times a week to make sure it's still there. It makes me happy even though I haven't opened it. Noah hasn't said a word – no hints at all. But if he bought it, he'll propose soon. He chose one of the more expensive stores in the mall, not just some cheap jewelry chain. Our wedding should also be unique and, more important, better than the one he had with Sarah.

Even after the two pregnancies, I'm sure I'll look better than her. For the reception, I want a tight white gown, like a cocktail dress, classic but impressive. For the ceremony I want something modest and respectable with no cleavage.

Just thinking about Mom's excitement makes me cry. The boys can be with us at the ceremony, and they'll be so excited. I'll ask Noah to bring them cute suits next time he's in New

York – three pieces with small ties. It will be amazing. And we'll invite all the guys from my small hometown. It's time for me to invite them to my wedding, since I danced and cheered at all of theirs.

What if Noah wants to invite Sarah and her boyfriend? That would be a little weird. I hope he doesn't think of inviting her parents and the rest of her family. She already got her special day. Now it's my turn.

The big question is what to do about Danielle. Do I have to let her stand with us in the ceremony itself? Noah will probably want her to be a bridesmaid or something, but she's a little big for that, isn't she? It's cute when little girls scatter petals, but a thirteen-year-old girl? It doesn't seem right to me, so I'll try to convince Noah that she's too big for this nonsense. She probably wouldn't want to be a part of my wedding anyway.

I haven't gotten to talk to her since the choking incident with Thomas, but on the other hand, we didn't fight either. She's even said a suspicious hello to me once or twice. Next week she's supposed to stay with us because of Sarah's trip, and I'm a little stressed out about it. I'm afraid to make things worse again. It's so hard sometimes for me to hold myself back after I see the dirt she leaves everywhere. I'm even afraid to ask her about her laundry. I never know what's clean in the piles on her floor. Some people cultivate plants. Danielle cultivates filth – and with great persistence.

Noah says it's typical of her age, but in my opinion, he's just scared of her reactions. The other day I bought a deodorant for girls and put it in the children's bathroom. I didn't say anything. We'll see if she gets the hint.

When she's with us, I try to listen to her phone calls, but I haven't heard anything beyond what I heard when she saved Thomas. What doesn't she want to tell?

I asked Noah, and he said that if she had a problem, she would have said something. I asked him to ask Sarah about it as well. She didn't know what I was talking about either, and I saw that she had written him that I was "just looking for bad things to say about Danielle, as usual."

"Stop looking for what's wrong with her," he said, probably quoting Sarah. Apart from asking Danielle how much money she needs and where to take her, he isn't interested in anything. To him, she's fine and we're fine. Everything is fine as it is. But from the part of the conversation I heard, I know that something bad was happening. Danielle knows something and isn't telling. I must know what it is.

I decided I would find out what's going on while she stays with us. I have a few days to try to figure it out, and she won't be able to get away with it anymore. I'll prove to Sarah that I'm not just making things up, that something is really wrong here.

I'm tired of people treating me like I'm a stupid woman, as if the better you look, the dumber you are.

According to this theory, Sarah must be very smart.

27

TARA

Surprisingly, I manage to bring the kids to school and get to the bank on time today to find debit balance reports waiting on my table. Difficult conversations are waiting for me as well. I try not to think about the businesses that may shut down and the employees who will lose their work after those calls. It's all part of the job. Nothing's personal. Pictures of the children from different times stare at me from the electronic frame Ethan bought me. When his image appears, I return to the piles on the table. I must concentrate.

"Good morning, gorgeous. Well, what have you decided about the job?" asks Erika as she storms in, putting the credit applications on my table. I need to get through them before my meeting with Jason, the bank manager.

"I don't know yet." I take a sip of the coffee I brought from home.

I've always dreamed of being a bank manager. Everyone says my chances are great, but with everything going on with Ethan, I have a feeling that maybe now isn't the best time for me to make changes.

Who would choose someone to run a bank whose husband

invested in fake real estate? How can I explain to them that I'm married to a moron? That doesn't say good things about me either. However you look at this, I come out badly. It's hard for me to give up on such a great opportunity, and the salary would help replace the money we lost. The thought of Ethan's mistake upsets me, and I feel hot.

"You have another week to decide. It's a pity if you miss out." Erika reminds me of what I haven't forgotten at all, but I have no time to think about it right now.

"I'll think about it during the weekend when I have some free time." I open the window. I need some air.

"With your four kids I don't see how you can have free time." Erika smiles and collects the forms I already signed from my packed desk on her way out.

I sit back and play with my necklace. I call Ethan's mobile just to make sure he's off to work but hang up before he answers. I don't want to hear more lies. He's been hiding in the house for weeks. People have been coming to comfort him, as if he's grieving. Absolutely ridiculous. *Just tell them you're an idiot instead of lying to everyone that Alex screwed you up.*

I'm debating whether to start filling out the application for the new job just in case, deciding to wait until the last minute before choosing what to do with my application – throw it in the bin or put it on Jason's desk. A phone alert from a news site interrupts my thoughts.

An indictment has been filed against real estate developer Alex Dvornikov for fraud offenses and suspected felony of disrupting investigative proceedings.

He just gets himself into more trouble. That's it. Our money is lost. I just hope he doesn't drag Ethan down with him as well. I call Ethan again; this time I'm mentally ready to talk to him, but he doesn't answer.

At this time of day, Juvi is usually with Emma at the playground, so I call Karen. Lately she's home a lot, which is not at all clear to me. She suddenly left her position, saying she's going to start her own business. She even arranged to consult with me on whether to open a business account – a little bit odd – but each of us can have her own midlife crisis. Maybe resigning is better than tattoos and a lover. In fact, maybe the lover experience is going on too?

"Hi, dear, how are you?" I try to sound as if it's just a usual friendly call.

"I'm fine. And you?" She sounds tired. What is she doing all day that she's tired? She doesn't do anything all day! When I last visited her place, I realized that she probably doesn't spend the day cleaning, and she doesn't cook either. It's also unclear why she's looking for a babysitter all the time now that she's home.

"I'm great. Can you please check if Ethan's Jeep is in the driveway?" I hope she doesn't ask too many questions. I have no desire to go into it now.

"Sure. No problem. Just a second." I hear her footsteps echoing in the empty house. "Yes. It's here. Is everything okay?"

"Yes. Of course. We'll talk later." I hang up before she can ask any more questions.

Is the window open at all?

I really need air.

28

KAREN

I end the conversation with Tara and go back to bed. I didn't want to ask her too many questions about the situation with Ethan. If she wanted to, she would have told me.

It's odd that Ethan's home all day, and I can't hear him talking and I haven't smelled his cigarettes yet. It's usually hard to miss that he's home. He also loves to loudly continue the conversation as he walks out into the street, always dressed in dark blue jeans, a black shirt, and a hat, always with a logo of a different expensive brand. In one hand he holds the Jeep keys and in the other hand a pack of cigarettes and a lighter (also probably expensive). No one can miss him.

I decide to mute my phone so I can really sleep. I don't know why I couldn't sleep last night. The house was quiet, and even Adam hardly snored. Although the conditions were optimal, it was a tough night. After an hour of flipping from side to side, my thoughts went to my parents.

Sometimes I think what my life would have looked like if they were alive. On the one hand, they would have been very sad that I'm sick, that I've left work and am having a difficult time. On the other hand, they would have helped me with the girls. Mom would have spoiled me and brought me things I love. Everything could have been different.

Last night I thought a lot about Mom, and I kept remembering her in the last part of her life. I tried to remember what she looked like before she lost her hair and swelled up from steroids, but I couldn't do it, as if the passing time erased the good memories and left me only with the bad. Then I tried to remember Dad, who became ill six years after she passed away. Some said the grief did it. I think it was just a brutal coincidence.

When Steven and I visit the cemetery, I feel strange. I don't feel like they're there, not at all. It's sad to see their names engraved on the stone and know that we're alone in the world, to know that Steven and I are all that remain of the family we grew up in.

Even in the rare moments I managed to sleep last night, I dreamed about them and woke up crying. If it hadn't been the middle of the night, I would have called Steven and cried with him because he's the only one who understands what we really lost.

The social worker at the MS center told me that she thought the loss of both parents caused the outbreak of the disease, and that the pressure at work only made it worse. Maybe she's right because while Dad went through the screenings, I occasionally felt all kinds of things in my body but didn't know with what to associate them. I also didn't have time to take care of myself with three young girls and a sick father. It was just too much. These difficult nights, and the tiring days that follow, increase my feelings of longing and loneliness.

Now the wheel can't be reversed. I'm stuck with this incurable, scary disease, a disease no one understands. No one understands what I'm going through. From the outside I look the same; on the inside I'm a wreck. That's why, when I'm asked how I'm doing, I simply answer, "As usual." How can I show someone that I'm tired, hurt, and weak, and at the same time continue to function as a mother? As a wife?

We told Jacob and Ilene that I'm sick a few days ago. It wasn't easy, and I felt Ilene's disappointment. Yes, Adam got a rotten deal when he married me.

"But you don't look sick. Are you sure it's the right diagnosis?" she said.

I have decided not to let this disease manage me though. It's true I stopped working outside the house, but I'm going to spend all my energy on being a mom, and it's a lot harder than I thought. I have no patience for them, and there's more shouting at home than I would like.

I also tried to learn how to cook. I really tried. I made a chicken stew but burned the pot. Adam scrubbed it for more than half an hour because I didn't want to throw it away and buy a new one. Now that I don't work, we should be more calculated with our expenses. If I throw away every pot I burn, we'll be left with none.

Almost no one in the neighborhood knows about my disease, which is better for me. I don't want pitiful glances and dumb questions. I don't want them to ease my burden. I love being on the committee; I love being a part of this neighborhood and feeling like I belong.

Adam sometimes raises the issue gently. "You left your job to rest, so why are you burdening yourself with the neighborhood stuff?" He still doesn't understand that doing something I enjoy helps me cope with the impact this disease has on me.

After a discouraging hour of lying in the dark, I realize I won't be able to fall asleep, and it's better to start my day.

"Do you want to come for a visit?" I ask Steven. He's been "between jobs" for six months now and can't decide what he wants to do when he grows up.

"I'll come in an hour," he replies.

I take a clean mug out of the dishwasher and make myself a

cup of coffee. From the window I see Rylie coming back from her daily run. How energetic she is. Not only does she have a stunning body, she also constantly dresses in tight sportswear that only makes her look even better. She raises the standard to an impossible level.

I move the laundry and lie down on the sofa.

I don't even have the energy to take myself to bed.

29

TARA

"Have you had lunch?" Erika asks and puts a plate of dry cookies on my desk.

I'll never lose weight if I keep eating this shit.

"Jason asked that you submit all the credit requests for your afternoon session," she adds with a smile.

"I'm on it." I'm so happy it's the last working day this week.

"Are you okay? You look exhausted." Erika looks at me intently, obviously noticing that something's going on. I have no desire to share anything with her. I just want this day to end. I want this week to end. All this stress with Ethan and Alex is killing me.

"No more than usual," I say with a convincing smile.

"Okay," she replies, sounding unconvinced, and leaves.

If I begin to talk about my problems at work, I'll lose my ability to suppress everything for a few hours a day, which is what allows me to continue to function normally.

My phone rings, and a rare picture of my mother and me appears on the screen. I promise myself to be nice and, more important, not to talk to her about Ethan.

"Good morning, Mom."

"Oh, hello to the busy manager. How are my grandchildren?" Is she trying to make me feel guilty, or am I just too sensitive when it comes to her?

"They're fine. How are you?" I take the first folder from the top of the stack and open it. It's not rare for a communication company to request a higher credit line, but these amounts require a more comprehensive examination.

"If you weren't so busy with your work, you would have called to ask how I was doing and you would have known that I was feeling sick all week."

I was right. She wants me to feel guilty. I can hear she's not home; maybe she's in a restaurant. She probably feels better today.

"I've had a busy week, and Emily wasn't feeling so good yesterday." Erika comes in with a smile and puts a cold cup of coffee on the table. That's really what I need now – coffee and an end to this annoying conversation. "I have to finish something at work. Did you want something specific, Mom?"

"Do I need a special reason to talk to my daughter? I want to cook the spicy chicken Ethan loves today, and I wanted to know if you'll come tomorrow so I'll know how much to prepare."

"I don't know yet. We'll see how Emily feels tomorrow. Now I have to finish something here." I look at the pile. It's going to be a long day. Erika understands she shouldn't wait and leaves.

"If you called more, then I wouldn't have to interrupt you at work. Talk to me tomorrow if you come and tell me how Emily is." She finally hangs up.

I sigh with relief. The conversation was relatively peaceful; I know that it could have been much worse.

Usually she says things like, "Maybe you should go home and be a mother instead of being at your bank," or "In my day, mothers were at home with their children, especially when they were sick." And the best is, "Why did you have four children? So that your Juvi could raise them?"

In reply, I always cite studies such as, "Children are happy if their mother is happy."

"Nonsense," she usually replies. "Kids need their mother with them. I'm not telling you not to work. It's important that you work, but at a normal job. You don't need a career. Return home at two and be with your kids. Their dad works hard enough."

Deep inside I know that she thinks that all her *offers* (as she calls them) are for my own good, but years of preaching, making me feel guilty, and insulting me keep us apart. She's a great grandmother, but over time I've asked her less and less for help. I want to avoid her lectures.

She would never understand why I have to work so hard. I never told her about Ethan's adventures. I knew she'd find a way to blame me – and my absence from home – for them.

She always defends Ethan frantically. Sometimes I remind her that I'm her daughter, that she should be on my side, but that doesn't help. Her grandchildren are always in first place. Then Ethan or, as she calls him, "Darling." And finally, me.

After Ella's birth, which was an emergency C-section, she came to visit and was only interested in the well-being of her darling. When he got up to get her a drink (yes, he serves her), she told him that he should sit down and rest. She made him a cup of herbal tea so he could dip the cookies she baked for him (cookies I hate).

I've really tried to treat her with respect, mainly to give the kids an example of how you treat your parents even if they annoy you. But there were times when I failed, and I hated being in those situations. We no longer visit her every week. Over the years I've lessened my encounters with her to the minimum required.

I check my tasks for tomorrow. Shit. There's a birthday party for a boy in Mason's class at the bowling alley.

"Hi, can you drive the kids to the birthday party tomorrow?"

I text Karen. "I'll pick them up when it's over." Karen always shares this burden with me.

Her birthday party is next Thursday, and I had been excited about this event. Now I'm less excited. Traveling with Ethan to a romantic villa? The thought of it makes me angry. Why should he even come? He can stay home with kids and his football games. I'll find a good excuse for Karen. I'm sure no one will miss him there.

I imagine traveling without him. Sleeping alone. Maybe even reading a good book. Enjoying myself with the girls in the hot tub with a glass of red wine. Perfect. I smile. An evening without hearing Ethan's stories. Without him showing off in front of everyone.

I return to my reality and to the pile waiting for me.

"No problem. I'll gladly take them," Karen answers after a few minutes and sends me a virtual kiss.

30

KAREN

My mornings are free, and it's definitely a refreshing change, even if it's been forced on me. I admit that it was odd at first to get up in the morning and not start the crazy race. Once I realized that I had to stop working, it all happened quickly. Within a week, I found myself at home. No chatting during the morning coffee break in the kitchen with people from the office. No lunches with my team. In fact, I now go on with my day without seeing any other adults other than Adam and Steven. It's as if I left the marathon in the middle, crossing the boundary lines and becoming part of the audience. Everyone goes on with their life without me, and I continue to cheer from the side.

My first decision as a free woman was to start training in the morning. The evening workouts at Rylie's weren't effective since I was too tired, but visiting Rylie is a kind of social gathering. It's nice to meet other women and chat while suffering together during the workouts, even if it's only two hours a week. It's better than doing nothing and spending all those days alone.

Since I stopped working, I've learned the real pace of the

neighborhood. When I was working, I would go out in the morning and come back in the afternoon. Then I would run around with the girls until evening.

It turns out that at around eight o'clock in the morning, the neighborhood is extremely crowded, which I usually missed out on because I left for the office very early. Stressed parents bring their children to kindergartens and schools, some by car on the way to work, and some on foot. I can see them walking with kids of different ages and sometimes with the family dog as well. Fathers carry their kids on their shoulders, along with princess or superhero backpacks, accompanying their children to school.

I see clear differences among the moms. There are the smartly dressed moms, the ones who go straight to their fancy offices. They are beautifully dressed, wear makeup, and all their hair is perfectly dyed to the roots. Their heels stomp on the sidewalk as they leave the house with a thermal cup of coffee in hand – like Tara, for instance. It's as if she's on the way to a fashion magazine photo shoot. Her perfect nail polish matches her earrings and, of course, her shoes.

I used to belong to this group, the group of moms that rush to the office. But I never managed to get organized properly, and I always put on my makeup in the parking lot of the office.

Then there are those moms who are in no hurry in the mornings, and they are also divided into two groups. The fitness moms arrive on foot wearing sportswear, like Rylie, for example. The other relaxed moms come in jogging clothes, which they probably wear as pajamas. Now I belong to the last group.

In the afternoon there is another rhythm in the neighborhood. Mothers drive their children from place to place, waving and smiling as they pass each other on the way. There are mothers I'm not sure I'll recognize without the window frame of the car surrounding their heads, everyone going to math lessons, dance lessons, playdates, basketball practices, doctor appointments. This is what I knew when I was working full-time.

Now I've discovered the secrets of the middle of the day, the late morning hours when the neighborhood is almost empty, when Sammi's is almost deserted.

I never understood how couples could get along if one of them didn't work. When I was working, I'd see those mothers setting meetings at cafes and tennis games at ten in the morning. I couldn't believe the day would come and I would join in. Life has decided for me, and everything changed in a heartbeat. My younger girls haven't noticed yet, but for Mia it was hard.

"What do you do all day?" she asked me earlier.

"All kinds of things. I have some projects, and I work out sometimes." I try dodging her question cautiously.

"Why can't you be like all the other mothers and go to work?" Mia cried, looking at me defiantly.

"Because this is what I've decided to do," I told her. I didn't want to share the real reason with her. At her age, she doesn't need to know the real reason for everything.

"You're really lazy. You're constantly resting and doing nothing." She threw the sentence like poison straight into my heart. "Because of you we won't have any money." Only then did I realize her motive for the entire investigation.

"Nonsense. It's not something that you should worry about." *It bothers me enough.*

"Because of you we won't go on vacation in the summer." This is one of the major problems of living in such a neighborhood.

"We went last year." I tried to calm her down a bit.

"Mason's parents take them for a trip somewhere every year. A long trip. And they have four children and not three," she said. She's always unhappy. It's just impossible to please this girl.

"Every family does what suits them," I said angrily, trying to end this unnecessary drama. "Now check again if you have any homework and finish it before ballet."

"I have no homework and I don't want to go to school tomorrow!" she said furiously.

Adam also has yet to adjust to the change. Yesterday he bought new cycling tights despite the fact that he already has two.

"Maybe we should avoid unnecessary expenses?" I asked as he came home with his new purchase.

"It's necessary. I need a new one." He put the bag on the table.

"And the new shirts that arrived today? Are they necessary as well?" I pointed at the package waiting for him on the table right next to where he just placed the bag.

"It's for work. And it's deductible."

"It doesn't matter. We don't have two salaries now, and you must start cutting our costs a bit. We talked about it."

"Okay, maybe we can start with the cleaning lady, now that you're not working?"

"You know we can't do that. It's too hard for me."

"It was hard for you even before you were sick. The only difference is that now you have an excuse." Adam went upstairs with his shopping bags, and I was left stunned and speechless in the kitchen. I felt the crunch in my throat.

I went outside, sat down on the front stairs, and burst into tears. Adam, the person who should be on my side, felt so distant. On the outside, I look the same, and even for Adam it's hard to notice that something's changed. I see his face when I ask for help carrying something or opening a bottle. People think that if they don't see a wheelchair or any other accessory, that everything's fine. It's such an invisible disease. Adam, too, fails to see it.

I wouldn't be surprised if now, after the diagnosis, he realizes that being married to me doesn't suit him anymore. Sometimes I see disappointment or mercy in his eyes, but I haven't seen passion or desire for a while. Once there was hope I'd feel better and return to myself. Now it's clear that it won't happen.

Ilene will probably also emphasize how sad Adam is and that he, her boy, doesn't deserve this burden – taking care of a sick woman at such a young age. Adam will probably take a few months to show he really tried and then let me know it's over. He might even have someone else already, a young, healthy woman.

I'll find myself divorced at forty with three girls and a serious illness. How would I even go on a date like that? And if I happened to find someone that wasn't scared off by "forty, divorced, three girls," when should I tell him about the "serious illness"? He'll run away the second he hears about it, and I'll never get a second date.

All I have left to hope for is that Ilene's horrible character will come to my aid, and she will tell Adam that it's "unpleasant" to divorce a woman in such a condition, and besides, "What will the girls in the choir say?"

My birthday is next week. If someone had told me a year ago that by forty I wouldn't be working, I wouldn't have believed it. Luckily, I've had this event to deal with lately. It's been a much-needed distraction for me, a distraction from everything. Instead of thinking about losing my career, I think about music. Instead of thinking about my failure as a suburban housewife, I think about the cake I ordered (don't worry, I won't bake).

In recent days I've been dealing with the last details: flowers, a private chef's dinner, and music of my choice. I took advantage of every coupon and discount I found, but after yesterday's fight with Adam, I'm no longer in the mood to celebrate. I don't want to see them all and pretend to laugh. I don't want to hear anyone else's troubles.

Mia sits in front of me in the living room with her phone, filming a video, doing strange hand gestures reminiscent of sign language. Her hair is back in a loose ponytail, and she makes faces at the camera. I smile. My rest will be over soon. I need to bring Amelia and Olivia home.

"What do you want for dinner?" I ask, but she doesn't even hear me. "Mia?"

"There's nothing I like," she replies without looking away from the screen.

Only recently, I've begun to understand how difficult it is to have a teenager at home. Teenagers are challenging, not to mention annoying. In a few years I'll have three of them. God help me. I smile when I think that if Adam decides to divorce me, he won't have a choice – he'll have to take care of them for half the week. Who said there are no benefits to splitting up a marriage?

31

TARA

Ella jumps on me enthusiastically the second I enter the house. "Mommy! We had a math test and I wasn't wrong at all!"

"That's amazing, sweetie." I hug her tightly and really try to smile and look happy. She deserves my efforts. "Where's Dad?"

"In your room," Ella says and runs back to the living room. I take off my shoes and sigh. It's almost my favorite moment of the day.

Juvi comes with Emma, who throws herself into my arms. I kiss her head again and again. Her smell manages to calm me down a little. There's nothing like the smell of a baby after a shower. Ethan compares this smell to the smell of a new car.

"Where's Mason and Emily?" I ask Juvi.

"Mason's at Jonathan's. Emily's with Ethan." Juvi starts preparing dinner, and I go with Emma to the bedroom.

All day I've been waiting for this moment. I want to change clothes and get some rest. Advil would also suit me now. I open the door to find Ethan lying on the bed, staring at a football match. Sweet Emily lies on my side of the bed, still dressed in the clothes she wore this morning. I'll probably find sand in my bed tonight. It takes me a few seconds to notice that she's sleeping.

"Are you for real?" I scream at Ethan. He barely turns his head toward me. "Why are you letting her sleep now? Now she won't sleep tonight!"

"What do you want me to do? She fell asleep." Ethan shrugs and returns his attention to the screen, watching the players run on the grass as if his life depends on them.

"I want you to wake her up! That's what I want!" I scream even louder, but it doesn't impress him much.

Emily's starting to show signs of alertness, so I sit down next to her and whisper, "Emily, sweetheart, wake up. Let's take a shower and eat dinner."

"I'm not hungry," she says, still sleepy, placing her warm hand on me.

She opens her eyes, which look just like Ethan's, and she smiles at me. Mason always grumbles when he wakes up. She always wakes up with a smile. I kiss her on the forehead and notice that she's hot – she's boiling hot.

"Are you completely stupid? Didn't you notice the child has a fever?" I kiss her again to make sure then put Emma on the floor. Ethan doesn't move. Apparently, none of this has anything to do with him. I lift Emily and take her to her room with Emma crawling after us. I dress Emily in her pajamas, the Hello Kitty ones she loves, and put her to bed.

"Emily's sick." I update Juvi in the kitchen. I put Emma in her highchair, and she waits for her plate. She has quite an appetite, this one.

"Oh," Juvi's constant smile changes into an expression of genuine concern, something I should no longer expect to receive from Ethan.

"I'll give her something to bring down the fever. Tomorrow she'll be home with you. Please try to keep Emma away from Emily as much as possible."

"Sure, Tara." She cuts the egg into small bites and blows on it as Emma waves her arms with excitement.

In my room I search the drawer, looking for the no-contact thermometer. In the background I hear Ethan's game and feel anger filling me. I find the thermometer and the Tylenol and leave the room as fast as I can.

I wake Emily up, and she slowly swallows the Tylenol without opening her eyes. She lies back and continues to sleep.

I return to the bedroom where Ethan is still in the same place. I close the door so I can finally change my clothes.

"I'm going to the casino tomorrow," he says matter-of-factly.

"Are you serious? Our girl is sick, you haven't worked for the last few months, and you're going to a casino?" I'm shocked.

"Rick invited me. What do you care where I go?" His answer is so annoying that I can't speak. His detachment from reality drives me crazy.

I change clothes and think. I'll have a few days off from him, a few days when I won't have to see his face. It can only do me good.

"The casino is on him too?" I ask after years of bitter experience.

"Sure," the liar replies. "We're also going to look into the possibility of investing in a hotel there. They're looking for partners." He presents it as a business trip.

"You're not going into any partnership. Do you understand? Rick can do whatever he wants. You don't sign anything." I know it's like talking to the wall. It won't help. I also know that if he does something, he probably won't tell me. I'm starting to despair.

"You're not my mom and you don't get to tell me what to do!" he says and gets out of bed. Apparently, he is able to move his ass. He goes into the shower and closes the door.

"Maybe you should go back to your mom," I say, but mostly to myself.

I can imagine him packing his new suitcase, the one he bought on his last trip to Italy. I can see him saying goodbye to the kids and going to his mom where he could sleep on the couch or in the guests room. His mom would have to send him to work every day and collect beer bottles and cigarette butts. She'd probably throw him out of the house a lot faster than I did.

I go downstairs. The children have already finished their dinner. Juvi takes out the bag of garbage and ties it up.

"I'll throw it out," I say and go outside. I also need a little getaway. I need some Ethan-free air. I stand and breathe slowly, taking in the clean, refreshing air. I hear noise coming from Karen's.

Someone I know from school stops in front of Rylie's house and goes inside. It's nice that she works and that the business does well for her. Noah's probably earning enough, and she doesn't have to work. Nevertheless, within a year, she has developed her own business. I put my hand on my post-pregnancies belly. It's time to get back in shape. I'll talk to Rylie. New future fantasies give me a lot of motivation.

32

RYLIE

"I'm going!" Danielle shouts and leaves for middle school without waiting for any reply.

I pretend that it doesn't interest me at all and continue to wash the dishes. My first workout isn't until nine, so I have the time I need to execute my plan.

Danielle's ten-day stay with us has just begun. Sarah's probably drinking coconut juice on a white beach in the Seychelles right now.

Noah comes down with Thomas and looks for his pacifier in the drawer while Aiden sits quietly eating his breakfast. It's the best time for me to get out.

"I'm going for a run now, babe," I tell Noah, taking Thomas's pacifier out of his bag. I close the door, determined to follow Danielle before she disappears down the street. Running quickly to the end of the street, I see her walking slowly, listening to her music on her phone. She doesn't notice me.

After the roundabout, she veers off the road to school and enters a small dead-end street. I peek at her from the corner. Danielle writes something on her phone and then leans against the fence and waits, every now and then looking in my direction. I hide behind one of the cars. It's a good thing there are lots of Jeeps and minivans in this neighborhood. They give me excellent hiding spots.

A girl who looks like she's Danielle's age comes out of the house, and Danielle stands in front of her, opens her bag, and takes out something. It's her purse. She opens it and gives the other girl some money.

I can't see exactly how much, but the girl takes it all and, without saying a word, goes back inside. Danielle turns and walks back toward where I'm hiding. I move and hide behind another Jeep.

She leaves the street and walks slowly, this time toward school. She calls someone. I try to get closer to hear what she's saying, but I can barely make out a few words.

"Yes ... I gave ... I'm on my way ... Are you crazy?!"

She sounds really nervous, but I can't understand what's going on. Well, even in a normal situation, it's hard to understand what she wants.

When she approaches the school, I turn around and start running back home. Why did she give her friend money? What's that about?

Maybe she's not her friend, I think as I reach the house. Maybe that's how she tries to find new friends – by buying them?

Then I remember. Since the beginning of seventh grade, things have been hard for her. Not long ago, the kids in her class shunned her and didn't invite her to an activity that all the girls organized. Noah and Sarah went to school together and met with her teacher.

Then Danielle asked to transfer to a different class because she had no friends. Again, Noah went to school with Sarah and they talked to the counselor. They went through half a year of problems with Danielle.

But today she crossed the line. Bribing kids to be her

friends? At my expense? That's too much. She could have asked instead of lying about it.

As I pass Tara's house, amazing cooking smells come from her kitchen.

While I'm cleaning the table, I receive a new message from Tara: "Is there an option to come for a workout on Wednesday evening? Half past eight?"

The message surprises me. She's hardly been here in the last few months. I choose a nice red apple, and between bites I check my calendar.

"That will be great," I reply, though I know it's likely to be canceled. If she cancels, I'll have more time to pack clothes that will look great in the marriage proposal pictures. Since Noah hasn't proposed by now, it's probably going to happen in the villa. There's no other explanation.

I think the blue dress – the one that makes me look taller – will fit perfectly.

33

TARA

Ethan left for the airport while everyone was still asleep. Mason and Ella were sent to school while Emily stayed home, lying in front of the television, covered in her favorite blanket.

I stayed at home as well. I decided that this weekend I'll be by myself and spend time with the kids. I won't cook, I won't host, and I won't go anywhere.

I play with Emma on the carpet in her room, and we laugh every time she beats the duck and it beeps. Who's the idiot who thinks that's how a duck sounds? The main thing is that she's happy. Her rolling laughs fills my heart with joy.

The phone rings, and Emma jumps and look at me.

"Hi, Mom," I say, preparing myself for an argument that's sure to come. I totally forgot to call her back yesterday.

"I hope I'm not interrupting your work," she says innocently.

"Not at all. I'm home. Juvi's cooking, and I'm playing with Emma." I'm trying to think of how to soften the blow. I smell that Juvi has started cooking. Whatever she makes is what they'll eat all weekend. I don't mind it at all.

"What happened? Are you sick?" For Mom, this is the only possible reason for a woman not to be in the kitchen, and that too depends on the medical condition. If you can stand on your feet   you can cook.

"I'm fine. I just need a rest. I had a hard week. That's all."

Emma continues to giggle at the stupid duck, and I lie down on the carpet beside her.

"That's exactly why I keep telling you that you don't need such a position. You need to be at home with your children and cook for yourself." That's her answer to everything – even complaints about traffic, or weather, or the price of daycare.

"Okay, Mom." There's no point in arguing with her. "Did you want anything else?"

"I just wanted to ask if you're coming today. All your sisters are coming," she says. She's not listening to me. She never listens.

"As I said, Emily is sick and Ethan is away. I want to stay home today." I try to bet with myself how many seconds it will take her to mention Dad.

"If your father was alive, you'd never act like that." One second. Mom quickly pulls out her winning card. "You allow yourself just because he's gone."

Yes, Mom. Just because Dad's gone, I won't come. Because Dad is dead.

Maybe I'm not coming because it's not good for me to meet the whole family. Have you thought about that? It might not be good for me to hear annoying questions like, "What's new?" or "Where's Ethan?"

Maybe I don't want to hear – for the ten thousandth time – how wonderful Ethan is and how wrong I am. Maybe I don't want to hear why I'm not a good enough mother, not dedicated enough, or working too hard.

Have you thought about that, Mom?

Maybe if every time I told you how hard it is for me, you would have cheered me up and told me I deserved someone better, you would have saved me years of suffering. Maybe?

"It's not about Dad at all," I say eventually. "I'll stay with the children at home today. If you want to come for a visit, I'm sure the children will be happy to see you."

"Maybe I'll come. You see? Sometimes you actually have good ideas," she says, but I hear in her voice that she won't come.

We bid farewell politely.

Emma continues to crawl around me and even stands for a few seconds. I hope she takes her first steps when I'm home. It will be the last first steps for me. Unfortunately, the odds are against me. I wonder what would have happened if I hadn't gotten pregnant with Emma on that trip to Tuscany. Would we have separated by now? Would we have divorced by now?

As far as my mother is concerned, success in life is to be a good wife. Keep the house clean by yourself and raise the children. By her scale, I'm a failure. If only Dad was alive.

If he had heard that I have an option to manage the branch, he would have been so proud of me – that's for sure. He wouldn't think that I'm a shitty mother if I apply for this position. He always told me that I was able to manage everything – not only one branch, but the entire bank. Well, maybe he was a bit carried away, but at least he always believed in me.

I'm smiling at Emma, who tries to go one step and falls on her butt. Why does she have to grow up with a nervous, unhappy mother?

She doesn't deserve it. Happy mom – happy kids, right? This is true even if the mother is forty-three.

Something in my life has to change.

After lunch, Emma falls asleep, and I take Emily to our bed with me and snuggle with her, sniffing her. My thoughts are running in all directions. What should I do about the new position? What should I do about Ethan? What should I do?

I hear a beep. "Mason should be ready at four thirty," Karen writes to me on WhatsApp. I even forgot about this birthday party in Mason's class.

"Thanks!" I answer and hug Emily. Her temperature is back to normal, and she even had some pasta earlier.

"Why are you on the phone all the time?" she asks with her eyes closed.

"You're right," I reply, placing the iPhone on the nightstand. I close my eyes. I have time to think.

What do I really want? I haven't asked myself this question for a long time. For so long I've lived my life on autopilot without thinking, just doing: wake up, work, buy, repair, help, cook.

All I know is that it's a never-ending race, and I run it alone. Ethan isn't part of anything that happens in this house. For many years he hasn't been here. He's like a bad roommate who doesn't pay rent and sabotages everything in the house.

I've never allowed myself to seriously think about divorce, but I'm already broken. The last few months have been too much for me. I'm tired of paying for his stupidity. I think about the kids too. Obviously, they'd be sad if we separated, but they're smart, and they'd understand later that it was for the best. I'm crying. Why am I crying?

Since Dad passed away, I don't cry. I allowed myself to fall apart the day he passed away, and then I decided it was enough. Even at the funeral I didn't cry. I just hugged my mom and my sisters. Even then I felt the need to take on everything.

I lie in the dark, hug Emily, and cry. I understand. I'm crying because something has ended.

I look at the clock on my phone and decide to give myself another hour of self-pity, and that's it.

Everything is clear. All the information is as clear to me as if I were looking at a balance sheet. I must cut my losses, and the sooner the better.

KAREN

"Adam, can you please take Mia and Mason to the birthday party? It's at the bowling alley," I ask because I can't find the strength to get out of bed.

"Sure." He puts down the book he's reading while Amelia is having her nap and Olivia watches TV. A much-needed quiet time.

"Tara will bring them back when it's over. Tell me when you want me to tell Mason to come out." I close my eyes and steal a few more minutes of rest.

"Tell him he can wait by the car in five minutes," Adam says and stands up, takes his phone out of the charger, and goes downstairs. I text Tara and close my eyes again. I've never experienced fatigue that lasts for so long, and sleeping doesn't help much. This morning when I woke up, I felt as if I'd finished a twelve-hour shift as a cashier at the supermarket.

I remember the nonsense Adam said the other day and manage to smile. He asked if I thought it was a good idea to renovate the kitchen and make it accessible. I laughed so hard. I told him that if I have to sit in a wheelchair, someone else will put the dishes in the dishwasher – and I won't do the cooking either. Maybe it's better for the common good to block my access to the kitchen now.

I feel a pat on my face and hear, "Mom, wake up."

"Dad's coming soon," I say to Amelia without opening my eyes. "Come on, wait for him here."

Amelia climbs on my bed, and I turn on the TV, switching it to a silly children's channel. She sits next to me and stares quietly at the dancing puppets, who serve as excellent babysitters. I must find a babysitter for the girls, and the hell with the money. There is also a price attached to our dependence on Ilene, which I don't want to pay anymore.

Today's fatigue is just terrible. This morning all the PTA members met for breakfast in the neighborhood café. Everyone was there, and I managed to settle the teacher's gift for the end of the school year. Then I did some shopping at Sammi's. And that's it. Adam even picked up the girls from school and kindergarten, an event they have been waiting for all week. So why am I so tired?

This feeling makes it clear to me what this disease means. I can usually handle it, but on days like this – days of insane weakness and pain everywhere – I can't understand how I'm supposed to live like this forever.

Adam's back, and Amelia runs to him when she hears his voice. We decide that he'll go with the girls to his parents without me when Mia returns from the birthday. I know Jacob and Ilene will be happy for the girls to come, and I'll be able to rest.

It usually bugs me to miss out on things because of this disease, but skipping this dinner isn't that bad. Ilene will be sure to find a way to complain about me even if I'm not there.

"What's up with you, sis?" Steven calls a minute after I write to him that I'm in a terrible condition. "Are you starting to fall apart on me?"

"I've been falling apart for a long time now, haven't you noticed?"

"Do you think the disease is progressing?" Steven asks, but he knows the answer.

"I don't know."

"Well, if you need something, feel free to call me. You're like family to me."

"Thanks, dear. I'll talk to you tomorrow." At least he makes me smile.

I close my eyes again and lie in the dark, listening to Adam trying to convince Olivia to wear the dress his mother bought for her as a birthday present. Good luck with that. Ilene's taste is not compatible with the one Olivia's developed over the past year – a combination of a clown and a princess.

"I just dropped Mia off," Tara texts me.

I send her a smiling emoji and hear the door open and slam.

"How do you feel?" Tara asks, and I hear the beep from her Jeep's alarm.

"I'm not feeling so good," I text her back, "but I hope it will get better."

"Stomach bug again? Your birthday's next week. You must recover by then!" Tara writes, and I know that I will never recover, that I'm chronically ill. Maybe it's time to tell her. Maybe I shouldn't hide it anymore.

After a good night's sleep, I do feel better and decide to take Mia to see a movie. I need some alone time with her, a kind of compensation for the last week. We argued about everything all week long.

The cinema is full, and because we booked at the last minute, only a few seats were free. We barely make our way to the end of the eighth row, and I try not to spill Mia's popcorn. I don't want to buy another one. Everything is so expensive in this place. I place the bottle of water I brought from home by her side as Mia sits down, noticing the look on her face that tells me she's unhappy. I ignore it.

"Here's your water, and hold the popcorn," I whisper to her. She starts to eat, still with a serious face. At least she's quiet.

During commercials, I check my WhatsApp. Something must have screwed up my screen because it's a little blurry. I hope I didn't accidently pour water on it. Maybe Mia's bottle spilled and I didn't notice it.

I turn off the phone and restart it, but the screen's still blurry. I put it in my bag and hope the movie is reasonable. I'll ask Adam to check out my phone later.

The movie is surprisingly good – another Disney princess sings and dances. No one dies, it ends well, and everyone's happy – everyone except Mia, who looks like Snow White's dwarf Grumpy.

"Now what?" She stops for a selfie with a cardboard figure of the princess from the movie waiting for us outside the hall.

"We're going home. That's it." I take off my sweater and push it into my bag. I walk slowly toward the parking lot, but Mia is still standing next to the princess, looking in my direction.

"Maybe we can have dinner in a restaurant, Mommy?" she offers and smiles. I turn to face her. This is how she manages to get everything she wants from her father.

"I'm too tired. Please, let's go home." I keep walking.

"But, Mom, it's just the two of us. Please. We haven't done this in ages!" She continues to pressure me but walks after me. She really knows how to make me feel guiltier, if that's even possible. "Let's do something. Please."

"I really need to go home now." I'm longing for the moment when I'm lying in bed and my body slowly relaxes. Every step is harder and harder.

"Ugh, Mom!" Mia says too loudly, adding a few stumps to get some more attention. A few people look at us.

"Next time, my darling. I promise." I try to hug her, but she pushes me away from her.

"I know you! There won't be a next time! You're tired all the time!" she screams, and her crowd grows. I'm considering selling tickets to her show, but I'm not sure we can compete with Hollywood movies.

"Don't worry, we'll do lots of things together, just you and me. But now I need to go home." I hug her and drag her with me as we move forward together, feeling that I'm leaning on her a bit too. My feet are heavy, as if sunk in concrete. The car is so far away.

I arrive home with a raging girl and find Adam and the girls putting together princess's jigsaw puzzle in the living room.

"Something's wrong with my phone," I say and leave my phone on the dining room table. I go straight to bed.

"Your phone is fine." Adam comes in with my phone and sits down on the bed next to me. "Was it so hard? What did she do?"

"This time it's not about her. I'm just tired of being tired." I close my eyes and feel like I've had a few glasses of wine, not one. My head is spinning.

"Maybe you should go back to your doctor? That doesn't seem normal to me." Adam stands up. "Do you want me to turn off the light?"

"Yes, please. We'll see how I feel tomorrow," I reply. My whole body is heavy, not just my legs. Adam leaves and closes the door.

I hear the girls rehearse for their performance. They make so much noise. Every scream pierces like a knife into my head. "Mom will come to watch later," Adam assures them.

How I'll manage on Monday when Adam is at the office all day. I'll have to take care of the girls by myself. I fumble in the dark and find my phone on my nightstand.

"Does anyone please have a babysitter for me? It's very urgent," I write in my birthday WhatsApp group instead of writing to each one individually.

I see Rylie is typing, and I close my eyes again. I don't understand why Adam said the phone was fine. Clearly something's wrong with the screen. It's obviously broken. When I open my eyes, I see that Tara is the one who answered.

"Still sick?" she wrote. "I'll look for someone. Don't worry."

Tara's the best.

"Do you want me to ask Danielle? She's staying with us all week." Despite all the bad stories about Danielle, I feel that perhaps I can give her a chance. I can't be too picky.

"Thank you, I really appreciate it." I return my broken phone to the nightstand. In addition to all my troubles, now I have to look for a new device. Maybe I'll buy one of those Chinese phones. They're supposed to be good.

35

RYLIE

I've been standing outside her room for a few minutes now, but I'm afraid to knock. She still scares me, this girl. I don't think she's ever been a babysitter before, but maybe she'll agree. I take a deep breath and gently knock. I'm coming in peace.

"What?" she asks.

"May I come in please?" I say in the nicest way I can, in the voice reserved for Aiden and Thomas.

"Okay." I guess this is her nicest.

"Hi," I say with a smile.

Danielle is lying on the bed, watching videos on her iPhone. The suitcase she brought is open on the floor, and clothes are scattered everywhere. A cup of leftover chocolate from two days ago waits on the table. I take a deep breath. I come in peace.

"What?" she says, as if every word costs her a lot of money.

"My friend, Karen, my neighbor, is looking for a babysitter. She has three lovely daughters, and she lives right next door. Would you be interested?"

"She'll pay me?" This time she even bothers to look in my direction.

"Obviously."

"Then fine." Danielle returns to her screen, and I realize the conversation is over.

"Great. Thanks. I'll give her your number."

I close the door behind me and notice I was holding my breath. It's unbelievable, but we communicated. That's a miracle.

Noah sits with the boys in the dining area and tries to make Thomas take a bite of the fish sticks Mommy cooked. He refuses, but Aiden enjoys his dinner. His face is red from all the ketchup. I kiss him on the head and sit at a safe distance next to him.

"Do you like Grandma's fish sticks?" I ask, and Aiden nods because his mouth is full. He's so cute.

"What did she say?" Noah wipes Aiden's red mouth.

"She said 'fine.'"

"Great. Karen will be pleased with her," Noah says proudly.

The truth is that after what happened with Thomas, I'm a little more relaxed to recommend her. I hope Karen won't hate me for it.

"What do you say about what I told you about the money?" I ask carefully, reminding myself of the little box in the drawer.

"There's nothing to say, babe. Maybe she owed someone some money. And even if she gave some money to someone, it's no big deal." Noah wipes Aiden's red hands clear from his plate.

It seems to me that it's not the best way for Danielle to find friends – and certainly not at my expense – but I don't want to argue with him about it, especially when the proposal is so close.

She can continue to eat sweets or pay off her friends. Whatever she wants. The price is small compared to the quiet it gives Noah. It's her body and her life and her friends. It has nothing to do with me. I'm not her mother nor her friend. That's not my problem.

If she needed help, she'd ask for it, wouldn't she? So that's it.

She'll take care of it on her own. Noah's afraid to deal with her, and Sarah's busy with her boyfriend. They're her parents, and if they're okay with that, then that's fine with me. I wish them all the best.

I just have to take care of my family, and most importantly, I have a wedding to plan.

I think the fall will be excellent. It's not too hot, but there's lots of light. My dream is to get married at sunset by the sea. A bit corny, I know, but it's the most romantic place in the world.

If Noah insists, a small wedding with only close family and some friends would also be possible. I'll invite Tara and Karen if Noah proposes to me at the villa on Karen's birthday. It would only be the polite thing to do.

All I have to do now is stay quiet and avoid fighting with Danielle until we drive to the villa. I don't want to harm Noah's efforts to organize the perfect marriage proposal, even if it means keeping quiet and tolerating Danielle a little bit more. I won't let her ruin my plans again.

"Is there something special you want to do while we're at the villa? We can split up from the rest of them a bit and do something just the two of us." I try to gently imply, giving him the freedom to plan.

"I don't know. I have no idea. Whatever you want, babe." He pulls Thomas out of his highchair.

"I'll think of something, babe," I say with a smile, and I shut the box of Mommy's fish sticks, reminding myself not to forget to give Mom back her boxes.

"You said Tara recommended the place and that Karen organized everything, right? So, what do you have to think about, babe?" Noah kisses me on my head and smiles his dimpled smile.

He organizes something, and he doesn't want me to get in the way.

He's so sweet.

36

TARA

"Maybe you should take a shower already?" Mason comes back sweaty from the park, and the smell is unbearable. Adam's such an amazing man. He took all the kids to the park to work off their energy, and he offered to let Mason join them.

Ethan would have never done such a thing. He barely takes Mason to the park; he probably wouldn't volunteer to take any more children.

"In a minute." Mason sits on the couch to watch TV, and Ella doesn't even notice he's returned home.

When he sits like that, he suddenly reminds me of Ethan – the way he sits, the look on his face, the way he ignores what I ask. I feel all my nervous tension with Ethan float to the surface and refill me. I can hardly resist screaming at Mason, so I walk away to the kitchen.

I pour myself a glass of red wine and go out to the porch. Karen's girls scream and sing enthusiastically. I have to think what to do before Ethan comes back tomorrow.

Why should I continue to pay for a mistake I made thirteen years ago? Why do I have to work so hard and then lose everything?

A wife should support her husband. I hear my mother's voice in my head.

I think I've been supportive enough, I reply, maybe to myself. *He can find someone else to support him.*

These aren't new thoughts. Over the years I've thought about divorcing Ethan. I've imagined living alone, only me and the kids, enjoying my freedom when they're staying with him. I smile to myself, thinking of occasionally having some time to myself.

Anyway, the joy of waking up without him in the morning, without seeing his face staring at the screen, without listening to his lies, without fixing his problems, is worth it.

The problem is that he'll be back tomorrow. He'll come back and pull me back down to whom I don't want to be. I must talk to him about this as soon as possible, before what happened after Tuscany happens again.

"Juvi," I say and pour myself some more wine, "can you make Ethan a bed in the guest room? I think there are things that need to be thrown away."

"Sure, Tara." Juvi turns to me and smiles. She understands.

I smile back at her. It's weird, but the feeling that she supports me gives me strength. Well, she knows Ethan.

My phone doesn't stop beeping from all the messages. The group of Mason's class is on fire. I go in and see a million messages, all of them about the science test. The main dilemma is whether the material for the test includes the subject of living environments. I had no idea he has a test coming up. I barely control my own living environment.

"When is the test?" I ask the group, and within two seconds three hysterical mothers reply: "Tomorrow!"

"Mason, do you know there's a science test tomorrow?" I stand between him and the screen, trying to win his attention.

"Test?" he asks and moves a little to watch the screen better.

"A science test." I move too.

"Okay." He moves to the other side.

"Okay? What's okay?" I lose my patience and turn off the television. Ella screams in response. "Just a second, please," I tell her, and she goes silent immediately.

"What can I do? I left the notebook in class." He shrugs. Again, for a moment, it feels like Ethan's sitting in front of me.

"Then get copies from someone. Have them take a picture and send it to you. Maybe Mia can help." If there's anyone in his class that knows everything, it's Mia. The teachers could teach from her notebooks.

"She'll never give me her notes," he replies, trying to grab the remote control from my hand.

"Maybe if you weren't bothering her all the time, she would help you." You pay for your mistakes, but not even his father has learned that. "I'll talk to Karen."

I turn the television back on, and Ella, who has been waiting all this time, calms down.

It's nine fifteen PM. The last thing I want is science, but it turns out I don't have much choice.

"Can you please ask Mia to send Mason her science notes? He forgot his in class," I text Karen.

She replies, "Noworries."

That's a bit strange. She usually corrects her texts. Maybe it's too late for her.

I regretfully empty the glass of wine into the sink and make myself a cup of strong coffee. When the pictures start coming from Mia, I drag Mason to the kitchen table. Juvi cuts an apple into small pieces for him, and we begin.

Mason actually surprises me. He knows a little beyond basketball. He knows the six plant-growth stages. There's hope. Maybe he hasn't turned out quite like Ethan after all. Maybe I managed to create a normal living environment.

Before I go to bed, I sit down and write Ethan a letter, explaining that it's impossible for me to continue like this and that I deserve something better. Someone better. I wish him all the best, and I ask that we go to a mediator to end it courteously, for the kid's sake. At the end of the letter, I ask him to find another place to live, and the sooner the better.

In the morning I wake up to Emma's cry, and the bed is empty. I don't know if Ethan's back or not. I go downstairs to make Emma her bottle and almost stumble upon the trolley that Ethan left just next to the stairs. He's sleeping on the couch in his clothes. Next to the trolley is a bag of his duty-free shopping. And my letter. The envelope's open. He read it.

Emily wants to go back to kindergarten. "I'll tell my teacher that I was sick," she says with unclear pride, jumping around me with excitement.

"That's great, sweetheart." I'm wearing my comfortable black heels. "Mason, are you ready?"

"I'm coming!" Mason shouts and runs down.

I look at them, and my heart sinks. I'm going to ruin the family of the four of them. Their lives are going to change dramatically because of me, and all the responsibility of their grief will be on me.

It'll probably take Ethan some time to figure out what's going on, and that this time I'm serious. I just need to be strong and determined, and everything will be okay.

"Why's Dad sleeping in the living room?" Ella asks, eating the toast that Juvi made for her. Her diet is really appalling. It's as if she's allergic to vegetables. Meanwhile, Juvi skips lightly in the kitchen, pushing lunch boxes into the kid's bags.

"Dad came back late from his trip. He was too tired to come upstairs." I look toward the living room. The morning's hustle doesn't seem to bother Ethan. It's a pity.

We go out to the car, and I see Adam put Amelia in her

booster. His car door's open, preventing me from opening the door to my Jeep. That's why Ethan hates this parking lot and always parks on the sidewalk.

"You don't live in a vacuum," I'd tell him every time he complained that the neighbors hit his Jeep with their car doors. "There are people here, and they have to get in their cars too."

"They can be more careful! That's all I'm asking."

Ethan whined like a baby who lost his balloon whenever he saw another small circle on his Jeep. Even so, it's the business's vehicle, so what's his problem?

Come to think of it, if I were a Mercedes, I would have gotten a lot more attention from Ethan.

"Good morning, Adam." It's only now that Adam notices I'm waiting behind him.

"Good morning. Karen doesn't feel well, so today it's my turn." He smiles and closes the door of the car. His hair looks like he's just left the barber shop, and he's dressed in a dark grey suit. It's such a pleasure to see a man dressed properly.

Mia gets in the front seat, not even looking at Mason, as if she doesn't know him. Mason doesn't really address her either, as if they hadn't spent time together at the park yesterday.

"I hope she recovers by Thursday." I manage to slip into the driver's seat. "Keep me updated."

"Sure. Have a good day." Adam smiles and gets into his car.

Why couldn't I have met him at the party instead of Ethan? I cast off the stupid thought and wave goodbye to him. Karen's so lucky. I don't understand what's wrong with her. Why does she need the tall guy she meets every now and then? It's completely unnecessary if you have a man like Adam at home.

While Mason, Ella, and Emily slowly buckle up, Noah comes out with Thomas in his hands. Aiden follows him and whines.

I try to remember the last time that Ethan took the children in the morning.

I can't.

KAREN

I lie down on the couch where, until a few minutes ago, there was a pile of laundry, and I close my eyes. The morning after the injection is particularly slow.

I wake up in a panic when I hear a dog bark. How is it two o'clock already? I put on my slippers and go as fast as I can to get Mia back from school – before she can claim that I forgot her again.

At three thirty Danielle joins me, and we go together to pick up the girls. Danielle's silent all the way – embarrassed, apparently.

"Hi, dear," Olivia's teacher says, and I get a surprisingly warm hug. "Olivia told me you weren't feeling well. I planned to call to ask how you are."

"Not so great," I reply and let go of the hug. "This is Danielle, our new babysitter."

"Nice to meet you."

Danielle smiles shyly and stands a little behind me. It's amusing because she's already taller than I am, so I can't really hide her.

"Olivia honey, Mom's here." The teacher closes the door so no child will escape.

On the way to Amelia's daycare, Mia is on her phone, but Olivia shamelessly interrogates Danielle, and I discover interesting things I didn't know about her. She learned how to play the guitar and danced for several years in a dance group. She loves math, and she loves to draw. In high school, she wants to be in the arts class. Definitely surprising. Rylie didn't tell me any of these things.

Amelia's fascinated with Danielle the minute she sees her and immediately acts like they're old friends. They enter the house hand in hand, and Olivia continues to investigate.

In spite of the short distances we traveled, I arrive home tired as hell. "I'm going up to rest. Will you be able to get along with them?"

"Sure," Danielle answers as Olivia pulls her hand and they go to play in her room.

I climb into bed as I am, with my clothes on, and my eyes close in seconds. What a relief to have someone here entertaining the girls without constantly telling me how wrong I am, that I don't clean the house frequently enough or that I chose the worst location for the broom. Yes, Ilene had comments on that too.

I haven't seen Tara for a long time besides accidentally meeting her here and there. Ever since I've gotten sick, I've had trouble connecting with the "healthy people" because they just don't understand what I'm talking about. I come across strange comments from people about my illness.

If you stood on your feet all day at work, it's not the same as the pain of multiple sclerosis. And no, MS is not atherosclerosis. There is some ignorance around this disease, but the most painful is seeing the pitying look on someone's face when I tell them, as if I'm about to die.

Last week, Adam's friends from the office suggested we join

a trip that includes hiking. As much as I'd like to do such a trip, and as nice as it can be to travel with other families, I can't now. They say the brain sees what it needs. I only see benches and chairs to sit on.

"What should I tell them?" Adam asked me. I could tell that he really wanted to join them.

"How would I go?" My fear of walking has overcome my disappointment with my body. "Go with the girls. I'm sure they'll enjoy it."

"Whatever you want." Adam tried to hide his disappointment, but it was all over his face. He could just as well carry a sign that says, "My lazy wife won't come with me."

If even Adam, who knows my challenges up close, fails to understand me sometimes, what can I expect from other people like Ilene?

Her craziest comment came after we told the girls that I was sick with a disease that causes fatigue. Ilene told Mia that this isn't a real illness. It's an illness of anxious women who don't like to make an effort. Because the girls were there, I held back and said that was inaccurate. At that moment I was ready to give her one of my injections that I get three times a week. I wanted to see what she'd say when she felt the side effects.

Toward six o'clock, I go downstairs, with great difficulty, to prepare dinner. Danielle's in the kitchen making an omelet with Mia, who smiles and giggles.

Olivia pulls plates out of the cupboard, and Amelia stands on a chair and carefully mixes eggs in a small bowl. "For my omelet, Mommy," she says proudly when she sees me. Even she has better cooking abilities than I do.

"Wow! How did you do that?" I ask. Danielle has turned out to be the surprise of the year.

"Nonsense. They're really cute." She smiles and turns to look after the omelet.

"Mom, look! I can cut vegetables!" Mia enthusiastically

picks up a plate with sliced cucumber, red peppers, and halved cherry tomatoes.

"Well done!" I sit down on the chair in the dining area and just enjoy watching them. Olivia sets the table with precision and folds white napkins. The table looks very festive.

"Do you still need me?" Danielle asks, putting the remaining eggs in the fridge. "I have math homework for tomorrow."

"No. I'll be fine. Thank you very much." Adam's due within an hour, and the TV will help in the meantime. "How's school?"

Rylie shared with me the difficulties that Danielle had earlier this year. The truth is that she mostly shared her difficulties with Danielle, but in between she complained that Noah is dealing nonstop with Danielle's problems at school.

"Boring. Stupid. You know," she replies after a few seconds.

"Middle school isn't easy," I say. "I remember it took me a year to find a new best friend."

"I actually have some friends from elementary school. My parents are just stressed. It's not true that I have problems with all the girls. Just with one. But she turns other girls against me."

Mia and Olivia eat as fast as they can so they'll have more screen time afterwards.

"What's the problem with her?" I ask, immediately regretting it. It's not my business. "You don't have to answer – only if you want to."

I clear their plates while Danielle organizes her bag.

"There's one disgusting girl. She's, like, really mean. Not just to me, to other kids too. She does whatever she wants, and even the teachers can't handle her. One teacher came out of our classroom crying because of her once."

Danielle takes her bag from the chair and stands at the door.

"Sounds like she's a nasty girl." I wipe Amelia's face, and she runs after her sisters to the living room.

"She really is. You don't understand how nasty she can be." Danielle lowers her head a bit and looks so fragile. I just want to hug her. She seems like she wants to say something else but changes her mind.

"If you want to talk, you're always welcome." I give her the money.

"It's too much." She hands me back a bill.

"Don't worry. We'll deduct it tomorrow – if you're willing to come again, of course."

"Sure. Thank you," she says and goes.

I stay at the door for a few seconds until I hear Rylie's door slam shut. If I tell Rylie how amazing Danielle is, she won't believe me and won't talk to me anymore either. Anyway, I have no strength to talk to anyone, so I'll send her a text message – which reminds me that my annoying phone is still not working properly. I don't understand why Adam says it's fine. Clearly, the screen is blurry. *Or is it me?*

38

RYLIE

"Thanks for recommending Danielle. She's a lifesaver! Goodnight!"

I see Karen's text while running and breathe a sigh of relief. I'm lucky Karen doesn't hate me. The whole afternoon I was stressed out. Danielle came home from Karen's and said nothing.

I didn't want to create problems or anything, so I gently asked Danielle, "How's Karen?"

"I don't know. She was resting in her room most of the time." Danielle took an apple and went up to her room.

This was our conversation, which for me, was a huge success.

I hope Karen's condition improves. It's really upsetting to get the flu the week of your birthday. In the meantime, the most important thing was that she was able to rest today. I hope she won't cancel the event.

I'm running home. The neighborhood's already empty, and except for some dog owners trying to secure a quiet, dry night, no one's on the street. Maybe if Danielle would be willing to open her door when the boys were asleep, Noah and I could go running together. I miss running with him.

Karen laughed at me once, saying that we're the only couple she knows that goes for a run on our romantic getaways. "You two are crazy. I would have stayed in the hot tub," she said, "but everyone has a different idea of fun."

I planned to pack running shoes to take to the villa and really wanted to run in the morning when the air's pleasant and clear. I don't know when Noah will propose, though, so I'm giving up my run. I think Friday is free, so if the ring doesn't fit, I can fix it on Friday. How long will it take? I'll probably be back before daycare ends.

I scheduled a manicure appointment. My hands must be groomed for the pictures. Tara recommended an excellent lady who works in the neighborhood near the café. Of course, she's more expensive than the others, but Tara promised I wouldn't regret it. Her recommendations are usually excellent.

This birthday group of ours has turned out to be a real asset. It's funny that we've lived next to each other for several years, and this is the first time we created a group for all of us together.

Tara is slowly growing on me. I'm sure she's not as tough as she wants us to think she is.

39

TARA

I return home from the bank with mixed feelings. Adam informed me this morning that he was able to get a written confirmation from the trustee that because no contract was signed between Alex and Ethan, the money might be returned to us. It's hard to describe the feeling of relief this gives me after months of stress. I feel like a weight has lifted off me. The option of selling Mom's house was spared. I feel like I can actually breathe better.

I didn't talk to Ethan all day, and he didn't respond to my letter. It seems to me that a letter will not suffice; it must be explained slowly and clearly.

I once again visited the lawyer that Adam recommended to me. I've met her several times during the past years, but this time I mean business. Adam didn't even ask who it was for when I asked him about a divorce attorney. Maybe he guessed. Now I don't care if he tells Karen – soon everyone will know. Ethan already knows, so it doesn't matter. Talking to my mom will be the hardest part – after talking to the kids, of course.

I walked around the branch today a bit like Erika. Restless. Jumping from one thing to the other. I worry about the children and their future. I fear their reaction. I have a million thoughts going through my mind every second. I could hardly concentrate on my work.

I'm at peace with my decision. Happy mother, happy children. The change will be difficult, but it will be for the better and all will be good in the end. One gets used to good things fast.

It's not like I'm sick or anything, God forbid. We're all fine. My children and I are healthy, and that's what really matters. Everything else is nonsense. But now I just want to get this talk with Ethan behind me.

Before I even get inside the house, I hear him in the backyard talking. The whole street hears it. "Obviously, dude, you're the first one I'm talking to." Sounds like he's back to normal. But I'm not.

I say hello to the kids and kiss them again and again until they get annoyed, then I take a few deep breaths and head outside to talk to Ethan.

Standing next to him, I debate whether to ask him to end the call or not. I just can't wait any longer. All the way home I rehearsed my lines, saying aloud the words that have so far scared me. Now I feel as if the words want to kick themselves out of me.

"Let's talk tomorrow, my man." Ethan places the phone on the table next to the ashtray.

"Hey," I say quietly, holding the words tight so they won't run away.

"Hello to you too." He smiles and puts out his cigarette in the strange ashtray, the one that Mason made in school. It looks like a monster mouth waiting to eat the ashes. By the smile on his face, I know he's heard that the money will be returned to us.

"We need to talk. Let's go upstairs." The kids are running

around the living room and kitchen, and I have no desire to have this conversation in their presence.

"Why can't we talk here? Come on, sit down," he says, moving his leg from the chair that's next to him. Really nice of him. A true gentleman.

"It's not a conversation for outside," I say, going back inside the house and expecting him to come after me. After a few steps, I turn around and see that he's still sitting there. This man doesn't understand anything!

"Come on up!" I say again, and he reluctantly stands.

"You're a stubborn woman," he grumbles, but he follows me.

He comes in, and I close the bedroom door. He immediately lies down on the bed, tired, I assume, from the effort it took to go up one floor.

"I hope you read the letter I left you. Do you want to talk about it?"

"What is there to talk about? You'll forget about it in a few days. I fixed everything and that's that. You see? I told you it would be fine."

"Are you okay? How stupid are you? I fixed it! Even now you can't tell the truth! I can't live like this anymore. I want a divorce. The kids and I deserve a quiet, peaceful home. It's not good for children to live in such a stressed home. We're not good together anymore. You're not good for me anymore."

Ethan looks at me from the bed but says nothing.

"You can stay here and sleep in the guest room until you find another place. At the pace you do things, it will probably take you a few weeks to find a new apartment. It's important to me that we do it nicely. If you want, we can go to a mediator. You're welcome to choose one. In the meantime, we'll separate the bank accounts. For all other issues, I'll send you my attorney's contact information, and you're welcome to find a lawyer and refer him to her."

"Stop your nonsense. Lawyer, my ass." Ethan sits on the bed and raises a dismissive hand in my direction.

"You broke me, Ethan. I can't do it anymore," I say, feeling the tears burn in my throat.

"Are you finished?" He's angry as he gets out of bed and stands in front of me. "Because I don't get all the 'I don't think it's good for the kids' bullshit. Who are you to tell me what's good for my kids? And what's good for me? Are you crazy?"

"The kids need me to be happy, and I'm not happy in my own home!"

"Stop your foolish nonsense! You're not a psychologist. How do you know what's good for them? I'm good for them." Ethan walks through the room, holding his head nervously. I think my words have started to sink in.

"I'm serious, Ethan." I face him with determination. "And don't say anything to the kids. We'll talk to them after we consult with someone professional."

"Leave me alone. You're crazy," he says, and I just want to throw him out the window.

"Listen, I'm not kidding. You have two options. Either you get it, or I take the kids to my mom," I say quietly and decisively.

"What is all this drama good for?" He opens the door. "I'm going. I'm going. Crazy woman."

"You drove me crazy! You!" I whisper and close the door after him. I shut my eyes and breathe. Only then do I notice that I'm shaking.

I go into the bathroom and wash my face. My mascara smeared, and I look like someone dressed up as a zombie. I clean my face as much as I can and then run downstairs quickly. *Just say nothing to the kids, you idiot.*

Luckily, he went straight into the guest room and lay down in front of the TV. The children are eating dinner and chatting among themselves. At least for a few more days we'll try to maintain a routine since their life, as they knew it, will soon change. Mason will need therapy, that's for sure.

I'm looking at my sweet kids eating an omelet without a worry on their minds. Mason asks Ella for some scrambled egg, and she gives him some from her own plate. What more do I need?

I notice I'm still shaking. I check the time on my phone and see a message from Karen.

"I'm sorry I didn't tell you sooner. I haven't told anyone outside the family. I have MS and I probably had a relapse during the past week. My brother will take me to the hospital in the morning for an examination. I didn't enjoy hiding it from you, but it took me a while to be able to share it. I hope you're not mad at me. I'll update you after meeting the doctor. By the way, that's why I left my work."

I'm shocked.

KAREN

During the night I realize that my condition is worsening by the hour. I can't hide it from my friends anymore.

I texted Tara earlier, and her reply actually moved me to tears: "I love you. I'm so sad to hear about what you have to deal with all alone. I'm not angry at you, dear, just ashamed that I wasn't there for you. I'm here for you whenever you need."

Steven and I quietly drive to the hospital, this time without any funny stories about our parents. On our way, Tara calls and we talk. What a relief it is to talk about it, to stop hiding it. I feel as if I've 'come out.'

I briefly describe my condition to Dr. Drew. "When I woke up today, I could barely walk. It's as if my legs don't listen to me at all. I'm so tired again and I have a feeling that I can't see well. It's been like that for a few days now."

Steven sits next to my loaned wheelchair and holds my binder. A faithful caddy.

"Let's see." Dr. Drew approaches me with his chair. This time he doesn't ask me to get up and jump.

After a few blinks in my eye with a flashlight and my failed attempt to get out of the wheelchair, Dr. Drew returns to his computer. "There's no escaping steroid treatment," he says, "and I want to admit you for a couple of days."

"What?" That option hadn't occurred to me. "But I have a birthday on Friday!"

"Happy birthday. Don't worry. By Thursday you can be at home and celebrate. I want you to repeat the MRI and start rehabilitation as soon as possible. We have an excellent rehabilitation center here." He takes pages from the printer, signs them, and hands them to Steven. "Take it to the nurses. They'll explain to you what to do."

"Okay," I surrender, seeing the shock on Steven's face.

Steven takes the forms, gives me back my bag and my binder, and rolls me out of the room. I never thought that at the age of forty I'd be in a situation that requires my baby brother to roll me in a wheelchair. It's humiliating. It's been months since I wore my high heels, and now I'm sitting in a wheelchair. Compared to Steven, I feel like Smurfette. How low will this disease take me? When I think about my birthday, I get even more depressed. To celebrate forty in a hospital – in a wheelchair? Everything seems surreal.

On the way to the nurses, I call Adam. "I can't answer," he writes. "I'm at the hearing. What's going on?"

"I'm being admitted," I reply.

"I'm calling."

While Steven deals with the red tape, I try to make arrangements for the girls. I write Danielle, but she's at school and doesn't see my message.

Steven gets stickers for me, and soon they'll give me the bracelet that publicly outs me as a "fall risk." As I see it, I'm already falling. Maybe even skydiving.

Steven rolls me toward the elevator, and I remember Dad's last hospitalization, only this time I'm the one sitting in the chair. I wonder if Steven thinks of that too. We're both a bit traumatized by everything we went through in this hospital with our parents, and here we are again – this time because of me.

The elevator opens, and we roll into the MS unit where I'll begin treatment. I realize that I don't have what I need for hospitalization and that someone has to gather things for me and bring them to the hospital. Most importantly I need my headphones so that I can hear the music I love and not interfere with anyone. Maybe I'll watch a series on Netflix. Anything goes. Now I have the time for it.

Tomorrow will be better. That should be my main thought today. It won't last forever. My vision will return, my feet will improve, and all will be good again, right? At such moments, I have to remind myself that there were better days with this disease, and there will be more of them. It's a little bump. It's hard to see it now because I feel like I see the world through a thick fog, but those days will come.

"We came to check in," Steven says with a smile, submitting the forms to a busy nurse. I'm not sure she understands his humor.

"Can you please ask Danielle to be with the girls this afternoon? I'm being admitted in the hospital," I text Rylie after I was discouraged trying to find Danielle.

Rylie calls me in six seconds. "Oh my god! What happened?"

I understand that there's no point in hiding it from her anymore. Anyway, if we cancel the birthday, she'll know.

"I have multiple sclerosis and apparently I'm having a relapse. I must be treated with steroids."

"Wow! I didn't know. Why didn't you say anything? Do you want me to bring you anything?" Rylie sounds worried.

"I really don't need anything. Thank you. I'll be fine. I just need to make arrangements for the girls. Ilene, Adam's mother, has choir today and she can't come."

"Sure. Take care. And if you need anything, please call me. I'll make sure that Danielle calls the minute she returns from school." Rylie hangs up, and I move to the armchair and wait for my treatment.

I turn to look around for the first time. The room is bright and spacious, surrounded by large windows from which you can see the many buildings that make up the medical center. On one side of the room are hospital beds and other comfortable armchairs. It reminds me of the room where Mom got her chemotherapy.

People, and especially women of all ages, sit on the armchairs attached to all kinds of bottles or bags. Some have escorts, and some are alone. Beside them are crutches, walkers, or walking canes, and some have electric wheelchairs. At the entrance sit a few Filipinos who speak Tagalog between them.

From Steven's stare, I guess he also has memories of difficult times. He puts his hand on my shoulder and stands next to me with my bag until I start my IV, then I send him to look for water while I listen to the nurse's instructions. She explains that a bit of a metallic taste in my mouth is expected, and she suggests I take off my wedding ring before my fingers start to swell. Lovely.

I'm shaking, maybe from the freezing room, maybe from fear. I might not walk again like before. I might stay in this chair forever.

"Danielle told me she'll come straight to your place. Who has a key?" Rylie asks and brings me back to reality – the reality that exists outside this hospital.

"Thank you so much. Mia has her own key. But maybe they can order pizza. I'm not sure there's anything to eat." It's so embarrassing.

"They can eat here," Rylie immediately suggests, and I'm so happy.

"Thank you very much!" I add a heart as well.

This is not a pleasant situation for me. This illness brings me to some awkward places. I hope the treatment will help and that I'll see and walk better. And that's not all. Now I have to let everyone know that the event is canceled. No party for me.

There will probably be a cancellation fee, especially since we're canceling at the last minute. All my plans are going to waste because of this unnecessary relapse.

I hate being dependent on others. I hate feeling bad all the time. I hate to disappoint everyone. I just hate this whole situation, but I smile when I think about the phone. I was angry at Adam because he claimed there was nothing wrong with my phone. I almost sent him to replace the screen.

There is one advantage to this hospitalization. There are three meals a day, and someone else does all the cleaning.

Have I mentioned no laundry?

41

TARA

Another business day ends, and not a moment too soon. Today went better. From noon, I was in consecutive meetings that definitely distracted me from other thoughts. I decided not to say anything to Erika until I know where things are going with Ethan.

I'm done going over all the transactions, so I check my texts.

"Do you know that Karen's in the hospital?" Rylie writes.

I answer, "Obviously."

"What will happen with the party?" she asks. This is my smallest problem. Rylie probably doesn't have too much trouble at her age. She's young, beautiful, and healthy, and she has a charming man and the support of her parents, who are just waiting to help her.

"I don't know. I suppose it will be canceled," I answer her, trying to think about when it will be a good time to talk to Karen.

I'm parking the Jeep in the parking lot in front of the house when I see him – the tall guy with the curls. He's leaving Karen's house with a small travel bag, and then Adam comes out and screams, "Hey, wait a minute!"

I stare in disbelief. What's going on here? Does he know about him? Has he known all this time?

The curly-haired guy stops and turns to Adam, who gives him a plastic bag, pats him on the back, and says, "Thank you, man."

What the hell's going on here? My theory evaporates in front of my eyes. I don't know who he is, but he's definitely not Karen's lover.

I don't know what I feel. Am I disappointed that I was wrong or happy to find out that Karen's not cheating on her husband – a perfect husband I could only dream of.

I walk into the house and take off my shoes at the entrance. What a relief. The house is unusually quiet. Ethan isn't in the living room. Where is everyone? I put the bag on the table and go upstairs. "Juvi?"

When I open the door to my bedroom, I see them all. Ethan is holding Emma in his hands while the children stand in front of him. Each of them holds a sheet of paper with a word written in Ella's neat handwriting. Together they make up the sentence, "I love you."

Ethan holds the word "Sorry."

I can't speak. The kids are so excited. I hug them, and Emma throws herself at me. They surround me and shout, "We surprised you, Mommy! We made you dinner! We surprised you together!"

"Yes. You did," I say. "Good job to you all!"

Ethan waits, smiling by the bed, and then comes over and slowly hugs me. With the kids this close, I can't say anything, so I let him hug me and Emma. I'm angry that he used our children to soften me, but it reminds me of our good times.

"I love you," he whispers to me. "We can fix us. I'll do whatever you want."

42

KAREN

"I'm not so well today," I share with Tara when she calls me during her morning commute. It's a good thing that I got a private room. I'm also getting the IV in bed, so I don't need to wander around the hospital.

"I couldn't sleep all night. They say it's another side effect of the steroids. The worst is that I'm not allowed to eat sweets or drink alcohol. Such a punishment on my birthday!"

"Punishment indeed. Without wine I'd go crazy."

"And my face has turned red and puffy like a tomato. I look like a troll. But enough about me, what's up with you?"

"I'm fine. We've had a rough time lately, as you might have heard from Adam, but it's more hopeful now." I can really hear her smile. "And with Ethan, things have calmed down a bit."

"That's amazing. I heard about the fraud thing from Adam. Sounds harsh. Tell me everything in detail when I get out of here. I don't know when that will be, but I hope it will be soon."

"What about the birthday at the villa?"

"I'll know for sure after Dr. Drew's visit, but I don't think it will happen."

"Don't worry about it. Keep me posted. I'm at the bank, so we'll talk later."

Adam told me when he called last night that the girls had such fun with Danielle that they didn't even bother to think about where I was. If it was up to them, Danielle could move in with us. Mia sent me a picture of a drawing they did together. It was truly stunning. Danielle's very talented; it's odd that Rylie never mentioned anything about it.

Dr. Drew visits and checks me. With huge disappointment I understand that there's no way I can leave before Friday. He promises that by noon I can celebrate at home.

"We need to cancel the reservation for the villa. Can you please help me with that?" I write to Tara sadly, adding a few crying and sad emojis.

"I'll do it!" she says after half an hour or so.

I feel sick, hungry, and sick again. I'm thirsty, but there's no one I can harass and ask to bring me something to drink. I go through the things Adam sent with Steven and find a bottle of water and chips. Thank God for small mercies. Adam knows exactly what I need.

"I cancelled the villa and all the extras you asked for without cancellation fees. I told her about your condition, and she just cancelled without a problem." Tara writes in the birthday group, which has become irrelevant.

"Tara, you're the best! And Karen, don't worry, we'll have time to celebrate when you recover!" Rylie writes, adding an emoji of a birthday cake.

The virtual cake gives me a strong craving for something sweet.

43

RYLIE

I return the suitcase to the storage room with disappointment.

"There will be more opportunities to travel," Noah said as he left this morning. I waited for him to mention the ring, but he said nothing.

I didn't schedule any more training sessions besides Tara's today because I wanted time to get ready for the cancelled trip. Nevertheless, Mommy arrives to help in the afternoon.

"The girl at home?" Mommy asks and puts bags of food on the countertop.

"She's been in the shower for an hour."

I glance at one of the bags and see that Mommy has brought more of Aiden's favorite fish sticks.

"Poor neighbor of yours." Mommy hugs Aiden as Thomas clings to her blue skirt with the purple flowers, one she's had for as long as I can remember. A "home skirt," she always calls it. "She's always so nice. I'll keep her in my prayers. Does her mother help her?"

"She died long ago," I say and see the sadness in Mommy's eyes.

"Let's eat delicious food!" Mommy smiles again and sets the table for the kids.

No one notices that I've gone upstairs. Danielle's door is open. A sticky glass sits on her desk, so I pick it up and turn to leave. Her iPhone beeps. She went into the shower without her iPhone. That's unusual.

I check that the shower door is closed and return to the desk.

"What are you going to do?"

The message was sent by someone named "Jen the blabber." I pick up the phone while she gets another message. And another.

"Do you think she really has such a picture?"

"Maybe you should tell your parents."

"Did you see the picture?"

Well, Jen is truly a blabbermouth. She continues without waiting for Danielle's reply. I can hardly follow.

"She keeps threatening you?" She adds a frightened emoji to this.

I don't quite understand what this is about, but one thing is clear. There is someone more horrible and monstrous than Danielle.

"Hello. Is Rylie home?" I hear Tara ask Mommy.

"I'm coming!" I put the phone right where it was and run downstairs.

44

TARA

"Is everything okay? We scheduled for today, right?"

Rylie seems a little scattered. For a moment I think I may have been confused about the date or time.

"Yes. Yes," she replies like Mason does when he's busy with his phone. I can see that something's bothering her. We go down to her torture basement she calls a studio.

"Let's start warming up on the mattress." Rylie points to a blue mattress, and I sigh and lie down on it. Rylie gives me a lot of guidance, and I try to stretch my legs like a ballerina.

"Did you talk to Karen today? How is she?" Rylie asks as I raise my pelvis and lower it back to the mattress. I haven't been in such a position since Emma's birth.

"Yes. She's suffering from all the drugs they're giving her, but she'll be back in two days."

Rylie gets up and brings me all kinds of other torture accessories from her closet. "Poor thing," she says, placing two pink weights next to her. "And on top of everything else, it's on her birthday. That's the most annoying thing ever."

"What's up with you? It seems to me that something's bothering you," I say.

Rylie looks at me a little frightened, as if I caught her eating a cheesecake or something. She bends over and whispers, "I think that someone is blackmailing Danielle. A girl."

"Are you serious?" I sit up on the blue mattress, and Rylie sits next to me.

"I followed her and saw that she was giving someone money. And now I saw on her phone that someone was threatening to distribute a picture of her. Do you think it's a coincidence?" Rylie continues to whisper and looks at me worriedly.

Who would have thought she cares so much for her stepdaughter? Karen told me several times that they're just like a cat and mouse, perhaps because they're almost the same age.

"I think it sounds fishy." My back hurts from this sitting pose. Rylie listens to every word. "Do her parents know?"

"They know nothing. Noah's in denial about everything that's going on with her, and her mom is with her boyfriend on some island in the Seychelles," Rylie says nervously. She really cares about the young girl.

"Do you know where she lives, this girl?" I stand resolutely and straighten my hair, which was flattened from lying on this hideous mattress.

"I think so." Rylie looks at me from the floor with a confused gaze.

"Come on then. Let's go. We'll put an end to this shit."

"Are you serious?" Rylie stands slowly, and though she's taller than me, she suddenly looks so small.

"Obviously. Do you think you can just leave it like that?" I take my phone and keys off the shelf and walk resolutely up the stairs. Rylie follows me, looking like she's about to faint.

Get over yourself, girl. You're the adult here.

"I'm going out, Mommy," she tells her mother, who is scrubbing the kitchen table to get rid of the mess that Rylie's boys made.

We walk outside, and Rylie, armed with her phone, hesitantly stands beside me on the sidewalk. She looks in all directions like we're going out for a robbery or something.

"Do we need a car, or can we walk?" I ask her.

"We can walk," she replies, and I suspect she's trying to push me into doing a workout after all. Before I can find out, she starts walking, and I follow her. We walk a few blocks and enter a dark, dead-end street.

"This is the house." Rylie stops at an old two-story family house. A faded sign hangs on the gate, the name "Sannen" written on it in blue letters.

"I think I know her mom." I ring the bell, and we hear the ring playing inside the house.

"I'm coming!" someone says, and the door opens. A woman about my age comes out wearing fashionable sportswear. Her hair is wrapped in a very tight ponytail, which is probably giving her a headache, but it smooths the wrinkles. It's rather amusing because she reminds me of an older version of Rylie. She stands upright and confident. "Good evening. Tara, isn't it?"

"It is. Good evening," I reply, trying to remember where I know her from. "And this is Rylie, Danielle's stepmother. She's probably in your daughter's grade." Rylie looks stunned.

"Ahh, yes. I think I've heard the name. It's nice to meet you," says the mother whose name I forget, and she smiles. Maybe I know her from Mason's class? I still can't remember.

"Excellent." I'm waiting to see if Rylie's going to say something, but she stands there like a mannequin and looks at me. I continue, "I'm sorry we showed up out of the blue like this, but we have a problem and it seems that you might be able to help us."

She looks at me, still smiling. *But not for long.*

"Your daughter has something, maybe a picture, maybe something else, of Danielle that Danielle would prefer not to be published. We believe that your daughter threatened to publish it at school and blackmailed Danielle for money. I'm sure you understand that's not acceptable, and given the girl's age, it's even criminal."

The mother looks at me in shock but doesn't argue. She probably knows what her daughter is capable of. Rylie nods (or she may be trembling, it's hard to tell in the dark).

"I find it hard to believe that Abigail would do something like that. She's very sociable and always gets along with everyone."

"Please go inside," I say, ignoring all her nonsense, "and bring her phone so we can check it and make sure it's immediately erased from her phone. We want you to tell her that if she shares the picture, we'll be forced to go to the police and file a complaint. We'll wait here."

"It doesn't make sense. Why would Abigail do that?" I know she's trying to justify her daughter's actions. She's not smiling anymore.

"It doesn't really matter why. Please go inside and get her phone, unless you'd prefer the police search her phone instead."

The threat works, and she finally goes inside while we wait quietly outside. Occasionally, a small fruit bat hovers over our heads.

After a few minutes the mother comes out. She holds a mobile phone in a unicorn case.

"I'm really sorry. I can't believe it, but you're probably right. Look."

She shows us the picture on the broken screen. It's clearly Danielle in the school's toilets. We can't see too much – we can hardly see anything at all, just that she was in the school toilets. But I understand why the very existence of this image would stress a teenage girl.

"Tell her we won't turn to the school or the police at this point, but next time we will deal with it with the utmost severity. She has just two days to return all the money she took from Danielle," I say and delete the photo. Next, I check to see if there are any more problematic pictures, but I don't know how to operate this Chinese phone properly. Most of the images were selfies of Abigail with her friends.

"And we also expect her to apologize to Danielle," Rylie finally joins in, and I smile with satisfaction. The little girl grew up.

"Sure," Abigail's mother says, this time without arguing. "And again, I do apologize. I didn't know anything about it. Of course we'll return the money."

She closes the door, and we stand outside and look at each other. Rylie can hardly speak.

The walk back home is slower.

"You're amazing. Thank you," Rylie says.

"Nonsense. The main thing is that it all worked out." What did I do? It's what I do all day at work.

"Thank you so much!" she says again.

We reach the sidewalk in front of her house, and she hugs me for the first time ever. "I could never have done it alone. I hope Danielle won't kill me when she finds out about it."

"Sometimes you just have to get things done and that's it. You don't always need to overthink stuff." I smile, thinking that this advice is excellent for me too. I understand that this is also the answer regarding the management opportunity. There's no reason not to try. I just have to do it.

"What will we do about Karen's birthday?" Rylie asks, continuing enthusiastically before I have a chance to respond, "Come on! Let's surprise her. We both took time off from work, right? Let's wait for her at home when she returns from the hospital and surprise her."

"That's a great idea," I say, checking who keeps looking for me on my phone. It's the house number, and I have three missed calls already. "I have to go home. We'll talk tomorrow and decide who brings what. And I have to make sure Karen's released on Friday."

45

KAREN

It's hard to endure all those long hours in the hospital. I wake up too early, and it prolongs the day even more. It's a lethal combination of loneliness, boredom, and endless tests. Reading is hard for me because I don't see well in my left eye, nor do I have the patience. I think the steroids are probably driving me crazy. My hands are also swollen – I look like a bloated red balloon. If Adam wants to leave me now, it will be perfectly justified; I'll have no choice but to help him pack.

I can almost cry at the thought of getting up alone in the hospital. Even in a normal situation, I feel so alone. I go over the messages in the birthday group and decide to keep it, though I realize the name of this group has to be changed. It's completely irrelevant.

We were supposed to drive today to the villa, and I totally screwed it up. The birthday celebrations I'd been waiting for all year have been canceled. It's so disappointing, mainly because after telling Tara and Rylie about the MS, I feel we could get closer and become even better friends. Right now, I can't think of doing anything.

I miss home. I miss Adam and the girls. I even miss their

arguments. The paintings they sent me decorate the ugly hospital dresser, but the girls barely agree to talk to me on the phone; it's as if they're angry with me.

The clock stands still.

In the late morning, Steven comes to keep me company. Adam has an important hearing in court and has been anxious about it for several days.

Dr. Drew moves the curtain aside and smiles. "How are we today?"

"Fine. I'm already feeling some improvement when I walk, but I'm weak from all those steroids," I reply, trying to sound optimistic. Eve, the head nurse, comes in after him, full of energy.

"Good morning. Is this your brother? You really look nothing alike," she says as Steven stands to shake her hand. "I see this one took all the height in the family."

"That's right," Steven replies, returning to sit in the visitor's armchair.

"From what I see, you can be discharged home tomorrow morning, but it's important that you schedule physical therapy for the next weeks right away." Dr. Drew writes something, and Eve nods in agreement.

"Whatever you say." I look at Steven, who shrugs, realizing he'll be driving me next week too.

"I'll give you a prescription for steroid pills. You should stop the steroids gradually over the next week. Come to me for a follow-up next Tuesday. All of this will be written in your discharge letter," he says.

"Yes, sir," I reply, and Dr. Drew looks pleased with himself while Steven gives me his "shut-up" look.

"Good luck and nice to meet you," Eve tells Steven, leading Dr. Drew to the next room.

∽

It's only eleven thirty, but I feel like it's been the longest day ever. The constant noise – phones, beeps, people coming in and out – doesn't allow me to really rest, and the nasty smell of the hospital is especially irritating. On the other hand, I probably would have rested less at home with the girls.

I have too many unread messages. Someone from Mia's class asked if it's possible to cancel the trip since they have a family trip planned for the same weekend. I answer, "Obviously!" This fits me perfectly. I send a message to the guide that the trip is canceled due to lack of responsiveness.

"I think I'll go home soon," Steven says, raising his head from his phone. "Is Adam supposed to come later?"

"It's okay. I can be alone. I don't need a babysitter," I say, which reminds me to send a text to Danielle that there's no need for her to come this afternoon because Ilene and Jacob volunteered to help with the girls.

"I'll go then. Feel good. I'll come tomorrow to take you home." Steven kisses me on the cheek and pats me on my back. These moments are always a little embarrassing for him.

"Thanks, and don't forget to bring me a Diet Coke tomorrow. It's still my birthday."

"I forgot all about it. Happy birthday, Sis." Steven leaves, and I'm afraid that he's going to hit his head on the doorframe, but he gets out safely.

"I'm coming home tomorrow!" I write in the birthday group.

"Yay!" Rylie writes and adds some flowers and hearts.

"What a wonderful birthday present!" Tara writes after a few minutes.

The group is gradually turning from my birthday planning group to a support group. It's actually nice.

"Thank you!" I write, hardly able to believe that finally I have a group of friends.

That's a wonderful gift.

46

TARA

Erika opens the door and says, "Have you had lunch? I was thinking of going to the new Italian place." She waits as I try to concentrate and disconnect from the hustle and bustle of the bank. It's more challenging when the service desks are open.

"I need a few more minutes." I'm completely absorbed in a customer's credit request. We've had a bad experience with him, and I can't find a way to approve this request. He'll probably need serious collateral this time.

"I saw you eventually submitted the application for the management position." Erika enters the room. "I'm proud of you, and I think you'll be a great manager."

"Thanks," I say, smiling, "I appreciate it."

"You've been working so hard for years and you deserve it." She walks around the table and hugs me. "Good luck!"

"Thank you, Erika. Really. A lot of it is thanks to you."

"Nonsense. When you get the job, we'll celebrate together. Ethan will release you for one night, won't he?"

"Obviously. I have to finish a few urgent things and I'm taking tomorrow off. I'll come when I'm done here, okay?"

"Sure, honey, whenever you want." Erika goes out and closes the door behind her.

This weekend I'll talk to Ethan again to make sure he fully understands the situation. I explained to him that as far as I'm concerned, he's on probation. My condition was that we try couple's therapy, and he promised to come. From my long acquaintance with Ethan, it won't be easy. He'll have to really listen to me and make substantial changes.

"Hi there. I thought I'd buy balloons and decorate her living room. Can you bake a cake? I think she prefers chocolate," Rylie writes.

"No problem, I'll ask Juvi to bake one. I'll bring wine as well. Anything else?"

"I was at her house yesterday and there was hardly anything in the fridge. Maybe you could send her home some groceries?" Rylie's idea is perfect. It requires a short phone call and a credit card. Completely doable.

"I'll take care of it. Karen said she'll be home at noon. Will we meet at her place around ten?" I'm never home at such an hour. It's crazy!

"It will be so much fun!!!!" Rylie replies, her enthusiasm echoed in all her exclamation points.

"I'll see you there," I add.

47

RYLIE

This whole story with Karen blows my mind. Why didn't she say anything? How did she deal with this all alone?

In retrospect, I understand many things now that I didn't before. Several times I saw her walking down the street, as if in slow motion. She also doesn't do anything at the house, probably from weakness. Poor Karen.

We must make her happy tomorrow. I spent all morning making sure she'll have the best day. I ordered balloons and a bouquet of flowers. It's going to be amazing!

Danielle comes home and stands in front of me, still wearing her schoolbag on her back. She's silent. I'm silent. I don't know what to say. It's so weird.

After a few seconds, I just say, "Hi."

"Did you really threaten Abigail's mom?" She asks in earnest, and I don't know if my answer will cause a third world war or not. I'm afraid to answer and weigh my every word.

"I didn't exactly threaten her," I finally say. "Tara did most of the talking."

"Why didn't you tell me you went there?" Danielle asks

quietly, looking at me strangely. I can't tell what she really thinks.

My heart beats intensely as I say, "I just didn't know how you'd react." I pray she won't freak out.

She doesn't say anything, but she approaches me slowly. Instinctively, I take a step back, but she just spreads her hands to the sides and hugs me.

It takes me a second to understand what's happening, and then I gently hug her back. We stand in the kitchen like that, in silence. She's almost my height already. When I met her, she was a girl, and now she's a small woman.

She releases me from her hug. "Is there anything left from Grandma Rachel's food?" she asks indifferently, as if she always calls my mom "Grandma Rachel."

"There's the rice you love." I stand frozen, still scared to make a sudden move that will make her burst. I feel like I fell into a tiger cage, and I'm not sure if the tiger wants to devour me or snuggle with me.

"Can you please get me some? I'm going to put the bag in my room," she says and goes up the stairs.

I stand stunned for a few more seconds and then walk toward the fridge. On the way up, her phone rings, and I hear her say, "You won't believe what she did! She took Abigail's mom down!"

I warm her the rice, still in shock from everything that happened a second ago. Mommy will never believe it when I tell her.

"Your food's ready," I call up the stairs. "I'm going to bring the boys back." I faintly hear something that sounds like "Thank you."

On the way to daycare, I call Noah and tell him what just happened. I didn't want to call him when she could hear me – didn't want her to think I'm too excited. I know that tonight he's supposed to talk to her. After what just happened, it might be easier for him.

I smile when I remember what Noah said last night after I told him about what happened with Abigail's mom. I smile an even wider smile when I remember what happened afterward.

"I'm so proud of you," he said.

"It's mostly thanks to Tara. It was stressful but also really fun. I'm full of adrenaline. I don't know how I can sleep now!" Noah hugged me and dropped me on the bed.

"I can't believe Abigail really blackmailed her! Lucky you didn't listen to me and kept digging. I don't know why Danielle didn't come to us. She didn't say anything."

"I think she was just feeling ashamed." I surprised myself by defending her. *Who would have thought?*

"The truth is," Noah said, "I bought something and maybe now that she's in a good mood, it's a good time for that."

He got out of bed and opened his socks drawer as my heart beat like crazy. He pulled out the small bag from Adler jewelry and my pulse went up even more. I felt like I was about to faint with excitement.

"I bought it to cheer her up a little. Do you think she'll like it?" He took out the red box and opened it. A Pandora bracelet with three silver charms rested on the soft velvet.

What a fool I was thinking he bought me an engagement ring. No matter what I do for her, she always wins.

"Of course, she'll love it."

Noah smiled with satisfaction and put the box, along with all my hopes and dreams, back into his drawer as I got out of bed and went to the bathroom. I wanted to cry with disappointment and despair.

"Then I'll give it to her tomorrow," he said in satisfaction, sitting back on the bed. "Are you okay?" He could read me like an open book.

"I really thought – or rather hoped – that it was something

else." I turned my back on him so he wouldn't see the tears that insisted on leaking out before I shut the bathroom door. What a fool I was thinking all along that box was for me.

"Something like this?"

I wiped away the tear that managed to escape and turned to face him. Noah was kneeling and removing from his pocket a gold ring with a diamond that couldn't be missed.

"Yes!!!" I jumped on him, and we both fell on the hardwood floor as I lay over him and kissed him. Noah rolled me aside and took my hand.

"I thought you'd love it," he said as he put the ring on my finger. It fit perfectly. "I took it for resizing. It belonged to my grandmother, who was a bit wider than you."

"It's beautiful!" I kissed him nonstop, and he could barely speak.

"I bought the bracelet to soften her up toward the engagement, but with what you did for her today, that will be enough." Noah lay over me and kissed me.

I took the ring off this morning and left it in the drawer by the bed. I promised Noah that I wouldn't wear it until he told her; I think that's completely understandable.

Mommy wasn't coming to help me this afternoon, but I have a feeling it will be okay, in spite of the fact that Danielle is staying with us.

And maybe it will be okay because she is with us.

Tomorrow, when we meet at the Karen's, I'll wear my ring. We'll have another reason to celebrate.

KAREN

The last day of treatment passed slowly with a small improvement. My vision was better, and the screen looked a little less blurry. In physical therapy, I managed to walk a few steps with the help of a treadmill. The main thing is that Dr. Drew is pleased with me enough to send me home tomorrow.

My birthday group has been renamed "The amazing neighbors" (Rylie chose the name), and the girls are sending me funny jokes all the time, which has really improved my mood. They make me laugh over and over. This is the first time since my mother passed that I feel wrapped in female sisterhood.

It's my last night in the hospital, and Adam comes for a short visit, bringing me more paintings that the girls insisted on sending, although tomorrow I'll be home.

"They wanted you to get up on your birthday and see their paintings," he explains.

"They're so sweet." I flip through the paintings and see that Danielle helped them a little.

"They baked you a cake for tomorrow, but by accident they used salt instead of sugar. My mother didn't notice. Be ready for it."

"No worries. I can hardly taste anything other than metal." I wonder if Ilene intentionally let them bake my cake with salt. At least she cleaned up after them.

"It's getting late. I'll let you rest and go rescue my parents before my mother loses her patience."

"Okay. Thank her for me. Steven will drive me back at noon and I'll see you in the evening."

"Are you sure you're okay with the cancellation of the party? We can reschedule." He kisses me gently on my lips again, as if he's afraid of hurting me. "You've been waiting for this for so long."

"There's no point. I feel shitty. It's better that we celebrate on another occasion, just the two of us."

"It's a shame ..." he says with a sly look, "because I made reservations for tomorrow for the restaurant Tara recommended."

"The one that you must book three months in advance? I can't believe it! How did you do it? And how will I get there? There's no way I can climb stairs."

"Don't you trust me? The owner is Tara's client at the bank. I talked to him and told him everything that happened. He arranged a table and the whole place is completely accessible."

"I don't believe it!" I cry uncontrollably, maybe from the steroids, maybe just from the excitement.

Adam sits down on the bed by my side, careful not to touch the IV attached to my hand, and gently caresses me. "What's not to believe? It's all taken care of. Danielle will babysit. Rylie just confirmed it. Lucky you found her."

"Yes ..." I can't speak, and this is definitely a rare event.

We continue to lie there for a few more minutes, and I feel the warmth I've been missing for the past few months. Adam fills me with hope that better times will come.

When he leaves, he takes the things I won't need for my last night here. My phone beeps over and over as Eve comes to check on me and take the latest vitals for today.

"Who's sending you all these messages all day? I'd go nuts."

"My friends," I answer with a smile. "They're the best!"

It's my birthday!

I get up for a birthday morning in the hospital, and Nurse Eve tries to discharge me as early as possible.

Steven rolls me in the wheelchair, something I never thought would happen. I mean, I've been scared of this moment ever since I heard "MS" for the first time, but I didn't think it would happen so fast. I thought I could manage it with the injections.

I planned to get up that morning in a luxurious villa, not in the neurological department, so I don't think anyone could blame me for being sad. The main thing is that I'm leaving this place.

Regardless of this hospitalization, my birthdays always remind me of my parents. Only when I became a mother did I realize that a child's birthday is your own celebration – the day you became a mother. Today I miss my parents even more than I usually do.

Steven and I drive across the neighborhood and pass by the little cafe, and the one who does manicures, and the girls' school. I feel as if I haven't been here for ages.

"Don't forget my bag," I tell Steven, and he pulls it out of the trunk and puts it on my feet.

"Hold tight." Steven pulls me to the curb, and we roll home. It's amazing to smell the flowers rather than the disgusting smells of the hospital.

I can't wait to be home, take a shower, and change my

clothes. Steven opens the door and rolls me in slowly. I want to speed him up, but then I hear someone shouting.

"Happy birthday!"

Tara and Rylie hug me, acting as if nothing has happened, as if there are no marks on my hands from the infusions, as if everything's fine. And the truth is that it's exactly what I need right now. Exactly.

"You're amazing!" I say when I can finally speak. Tara holds my hand.

The entire living room is decorated with colorful balloons. The digits "40" hover in the center of the room, and Rylie puts a flower crown on my head. A cake with candles awaits me on the table, and it doesn't look like something the girls made, thank goodness. A huge bouquet of flowers stands on the dining table next to the cake, plus a few smaller bouquets are scattered throughout the living room. It all looks amazing.

Steven stands behind me, maybe a little pleased that no one is referring to him.

"Steven, these are my friends – Tara and Rylie. They live next door. And this is Steven, my little brother."

"Nice to meet you," Tara says, with her big smile. "You don't look alike."

Only now do I notice she's wearing dark-blue jeans and a white T- shirt. This is the first time I've seen her in jeans. She looks much younger.

"It's nice to meet you." Rylie shakes hands with Steven. Are Rylie and Tara exchanging glances? Maybe I'm just imagining it.

"I'll go now, I think," Steven says. "Happy birthday, Sis." He gives me a kiss on the cheek and leaves.

"Come on. Let's get out to the yard. Are you allowed to drink sangria?" Tara rolls me out without waiting for my answer.

We go through the living room, and I notice that the house

is neat – there's not one crayon in the living room, nor any laundry either.

"I don't think I'm allowed to, but who's going to tell?" I lock the wheels as we stop, and Rylie pours me a glass of sangria. The smell is intoxicating.

They help me move to a standard chair and throw the wheelchair aside. I feel almost normal.

Everyone's glasses are full, and Tara says, "To Karen!" We launch them together, smiling and happy, and for a moment I forget about everything – the wheelchair, the steroids that inflated me like a balloon, and the longing for my parents.

A ring at the front door interrupts Rylie from continuing her story about Danielle and the proposal. Tara opens the door.

"You can lay it here," I hear Tara say, and I peep inside to see who she's talking with. Sammi from the grocery store comes in with a box full of groceries and puts it on the table. He looks around and waves to me as soon as he notices me in the garden.

"Happy birthday!" he says loudly from the kitchen.

"Thanks, Sammi," I say with a smile, feeling a little silly with the crown on my head. He looks a little embarrassed too.

"Enjoy yourselves, ladies," he says.

"Don't you want to sit with us for a bit? We have tons of sangria," Tara says, surprising me, and probably Sammi too.

"I wish I could, believe me. I must go back to the grocery store. Don will kill me if I ask for help with the deliveries," he says, but he approaches us. "Believe me when I say that I'd happily change places with you. Sitting here between the trees with a cocktail in hand. Not too bad. Not bad at all."

"Come on and have a toast with us. We celebrate forty today!" Tara pours him half a glass of sangria, and Sammi embarrassedly approaches the table.

"And an engagement too!" Rylie adds with enthusiasm and shows him the ring.

"Congratulations to you both!" he says and tastes a little of the sangria. "How nice that you can have this time together. I always say that the most important things in life are health and good friends."

"You're so right!" I say, trying to remember how I celebrated last year's birthday, but I can't.

"I'm sorry ladies but I must go now. Congratulations!" Sammi says, taking one more look before he places the glass on the table and walks away. "Your life is good as gold, I tell you. Good as gold."

AUTHOR'S NOTE

If you haven't read *A Part Of Me* - A Gripping Emotional Page Turning Novel, Based on a True Story of a Breast Cancer Previvor - By Karin Aharon, you can get it here: A Part of Me

Printed in Great Britain
by Amazon

78888939R00135